Twenty-Two Goblins

Twenty-Two Goblins

Translated from the Sanskrit by Arthur W. Ryder

INTRODUCTION

On the bank of the Godavari River is a kingdom called the Abiding Kingdom. There lived the son of King Victory, the famous King Triple-victory, mighty as the king of the gods. As this king sat in judgment, a monk called Patience brought him every day one piece of fruit as an expression of homage. And the king took it and gave it each day to the treasurer who stood near. Thus twelve years passed.

Now one day the monk came to court, gave the king a piece of fruit as usual, and went away. But on this day the king gave the fruit to a pet baby monkey that had escaped from his keepers, and happened to wander in. And as the monkey ate the fruit, he split it open, and a priceless, magnificent gem came out.

When the king saw this, he took it and asked the treasurer: "Where have you been keeping the fruits which the monk brought? I gave them to you." When the treasurer heard this, he was frightened and said: "Your Majesty, I have thrown them all through the window. If your Majesty desires, I will look for them now." And when the king had dismissed him, he went, but returned in a moment, and said again: "Your Majesty, they were all smashed in the treasury, and in them I see heaps of dazzling gems."

When he heard this, the king was delighted, and gave the jewels to the treasurer. And when the monk came the next day, he asked him: "Monk, why do you keep honouring me in such an expensive way? Unless I know the reason, I will not take your fruit."

Then the monk took the king aside and said: "O hero, there is a business in which I need help. So I ask for your help in it, because you are a brave man." And the king promised his assistance.

Then the monk was pleased, and said again: "O King, on the last night of the waning moon, you must go to the great cemetery at nightfall, and come to me under the fig-tree." Then the king said "Certainly," and Patience, the monk, went home well pleased.

So when the night came, the mighty king remembered his promise to the monk, and at dusk he wrapped his head in a black veil, took his sword in his hand, and went to the great cemetery without being seen. When he got there, he looked about, and saw the monk standing under the fig-tree and making a magic circle. So he went up and said: "Monk, here I am. Tell me what I am to do for you."

And when the monk saw the king, he was delighted and said: "O King, if you wish to do me a favour, go south from here some distance all alone, and you will see a sissoo tree and a dead body hanging from it. Be so kind as to bring that here."

When the brave king heard this, he agreed, and, true to his promise, turned south and started. And as he walked with difficulty along the cemetery road, he came upon the sissoo tree at some distance, and saw a body hanging on it. So he climbed the tree, cut the rope, and let it fall to the ground. And as it fell, it unexpectedly cried aloud, as if alive. Then the king climbed down, and thinking it was alive, he mercifully rubbed its limbs. Then the body gave a loud laugh.

So the king knew that a goblin lived in it, and said without fear: "What are you laughing about? Come, let us be off." But then he did not see the goblin on the ground any longer. And when he looked up, there he was, hanging in the tree as before. So the king climbed the tree again, and carefully carried the body down. A brave man's heart is harder than a diamond, and nothing makes it tremble.

Then he put the body with the goblin in it on his shoulder, and started off in silence. And as he walked along, the goblin in the body said: "O King, to amuse the journey, I will tell you a story. Listen."

The Prince's Elopement
Whose fault was the resulting death of his parents-in-law?

There is a city called Benares where Shiva lives. It is loved by pious people like the soil of Mount Kailasa. The river of heaven shines there like a pearl necklace. And in the city lived a king called Valour who burned up all his enemies by his valour, as a fire burns a forest. He had a son named Thunderbolt who broke the pride of the love-god by his beauty, and the pride of men by his bravery. This prince had a clever friend, the son of a counsellor.

One day the prince was enjoying himself with his friend hunting, and went a long distance. And so he came to a great forest. There he saw a beautiful lake, and being tired, he drank from it with his friend the counsellor's son, washed his hands and feet, and sat down under a tree on the bank.

And then he saw a beautiful maiden who had come there with her servants to bathe. She seemed to fill the lake with the stream of her beauty, and seemed to make lilies grow there with her eyes, and seemed to shame the lotuses with a face more lovely than the moon. She captured the prince's heart the moment that he saw her. And the prince took her eyes captive.

The girl had a strange feeling when she saw him, but was too modest to say a word. So she gave a hint of the feeling in her heart. She put a lotus on her ear, laid a lily on her head after she had made the edge look like a row of teeth, and placed her hand on her heart. But the prince did not understand her signs, only the clever counsellor's son understood them all.

A moment later the girl went away, led by her servants. She went home and sat on the sofa and stayed there. But her thoughts were with the prince.

The prince went slowly back to his city, and was terribly lonely without her, and grew thinner every day. Then his friend the son of the counsellor took him aside and told him

that she was not hard to find. But he had lost all courage and
said: "My friend, I don't know her name, nor her home, nor
her family. How can I find her? Why do you vainly try to
comfort me?"

Then the counsellor's son said: "Did you not see all that she
hinted with her signs? When she put the lotus on her ear, she
meant that she lived in the kingdom of a king named
Ear-lotus. And when she made the row of teeth, she meant
that she was the daughter of a man named Bite there. And
when she laid the lily on her head, she meant that her name
was Lily. And when she placed her hand on her heart, she
meant that she loved you. And there is a king named
Ear-lotus in the Kalinga country. There is a very rich man
there whom the king likes. His real name is Battler, but they
call him Bite. He has a pearl of a girl whom he loves more
than his life, and her name is Lily. This is true, because
people told me. So I understood her signs about her country
and the other things." When the counsellor's son had said
this, the prince was delighted to find him so clever, and
pleased because he knew what to do.

Then he formed a plan with the counsellor's son, and
started for the lake again, pretending that he was going to
hunt, but really to find the girl that he loved. On the way he
rode like the wind away from his soldiers, and started for the
Kalinga country with the counsellor's son.

When they reached the city of King Ear-lotus, they looked
about and found the house of the man called Bite, and they
went to a house near by to live with an old woman. And the
counsellor's son said to the old woman: "Old woman, do you
know anybody named Bite in this city?"

Then the old woman answered him respectfully: "My son,
I know him well. I was his nurse. And I am a servant of his
daughter Lily. But I do not go there now because my dress is
stolen. My naughty son is a gambler and steals my clothes."

Then the counsellor's son was pleased and satisfied her
with his own cloak and other presents. And he said: "Mother,
you must do very secretly what we tell you. Go to Bite's
daughter Lily, and tell her that the prince whom she saw on

the bank of the lake is here, and sent you with a love-message to her."

The old woman was pleased with the gifts and went to Lily at once. And when she got a chance, she said: "My child, the prince and the counsellor's son have come to take you. Tell me what to do now." But the girl scolded her and struck her cheeks with both hands smeared with camphor.

The old woman was hurt by this treatment, and came home weeping, and said to the two men: "My sons, see how she left the marks of her fingers on my face."

And the prince was hopeless and sad, but the very clever counsellor's son took him aside and said, "My friend, do not be sad. She was only keeping the secret when she scolded the old woman, and put ten fingers white with camphor on her face. She meant that you must wait before seeing her, for the next ten nights are bright with moonlight."

So the counsellor's son comforted the prince, took a little gold ornament and sold it in the market, and bought a great dinner for the old woman. So they two took dinner with the old woman. They did this for ten days, and then the counsellor's son sent her to Lily again, to find out something more.

And the old woman was eager for dainty food and drink. So to please him she went to Lily's house, and then came back and said: "My children, I went there and stayed with her for some time without speaking. But she spoke herself of my naughtiness in mentioning you, and struck me again on the chest with three fingers stained red. So I came back in disgrace."

Then the counsellor's son whispered to the prince: "Don't be alarmed, my friend. When she left the marks of three red fingers on the old woman's heart, she meant to say very cleverly that there were three dangerous days coming." So the counsellor's son comforted the prince.

And when three days were gone, he sent the old woman to Lily again. And this time she went and was very respectfully entertained, and treated to wine and other things the whole day. But when she was ready to go back in the evening, a terrible shouting was heard outside. They heard people running and crying: "Oh, oh! A mad elephant has escaped from his stable and is running around and stamping on people."

Then Lily said to the old woman: "Mother, you must not go through the street now where the elephant is. I will put you in a swing and let you down with ropes through this great window into the garden. Then you can climb into a tree and jump on the wall, and go home by way of another tree." So she had her servants let the old woman down from the window into the garden by a rope-swing. And the old woman went home and told the prince and the counsellor's son all about it.

Then the counsellor's son said to the prince: "My friend, your wishes are fulfilled. She has been clever enough to show you the road. So you must follow that same road this very evening to the room of your darling."

So the prince went to the garden with the counsellor's son by the road that the old woman had shown them. And there he saw the rope-swing hanging down, and servants above keeping an eye on the road. And when he got into the swing, the servants at the window pulled at the rope and he came to his darling. And when he had gone in, the counsellor's son went back to the old woman's house.

But the prince saw Lily, and her face was beautiful like the full moon, and the moonlight of her beauty shone forth, like the night when the moon shines in secret because of the dark. And when she saw him, she threw her arms around his neck and kissed him. So he married her and stayed hidden with her for some days.

One day he said to his wife: "My dear, my friend the counsellor's son came with me, and he is staying all alone at the old woman's house. I must go and see him, then I will come back."

But Lily was shrewd and said: "My dear, I must ask you something. Did you understand the signs I made, or was it the counsellor's son?" And the prince said to her: "My dear, I did not understand them all, but my friend has wonderful wisdom. He understood everything and told me." Then the sweet girl thought, and said: "My dear, you did wrong not to tell me before. Your friend is a real brother to me. I ought to have sent him some nuts and other nice things at the very first."

Then she let him go, and he went to his friend by night by the same road, and told all that his wife had said. But the counsellor's son said: "That is foolish," and did not think much of it. So they spent the night talking.

Then when the time for the twilight sacrifice came, a friend of Lily's came there with cooked rice and nuts in her hand. She came and asked the counsellor's son about his health and gave him the present. And she cleverly tried to keep the prince from eating. "Your wife is expecting you to dinner," she said, and a moment later she went away.

Then the counsellor's son said to the prince: "Look, your Majesty. I will show you something curious." So he took a little of the cooked rice and gave it to a dog that was there. And the moment he ate it, the dog died. And the prince asked the counsellor's son what this strange thing could mean.

And he replied: "Your Majesty, she knew that I was clever because I understood her signs, and she wanted to kill me out of love for you. For she thought the prince would not be all her own while I was alive, but would leave her for my sake and go back to his own city. So she sent me poisoned food to eat. But you must not be angry with her. I will think up some scheme."

Then the prince praised the counsellor's son, and said: "You are truly the body of wisdom." And then suddenly a great wailing of grief-stricken people was heard: "Alas! Alas! The king's little son is dead."

When he heard this, the counsellor's son was delighted, and said: "Your Majesty, go to-night to Lily's house, and make her drink wine until she loses her senses and seems to be dead. Then as she lies there, make a mark on her hip with a red-hot fork, steal her jewels, and come back the old way through the window. After that I will do the right thing."

Then he made a three-pronged fork and gave it to the prince. And the prince took the crooked, cruel thing, hard as the weapon of Death, and went by night as before to Lily's house. "A king," he thought, "ought not to disregard the words of a high- minded counsellor." So when he had stupefied her with wine, he branded her hip with the fork, stole her jewels, returned to his friend, and told him everything, showing him the jewels.

Then the counsellor's son felt sure his scheme was successful. He went to the cemetery in the morning, and disguised himself as a hermit, and the prince as his pupil. And he said: "Take this pearl necklace from among the jewels. Go and sell it in the market-place. And if the policemen arrest you, say this: It was given to me to sell by my teacher.'"

So the prince went to the market-place and stood there offering the pearl necklace for sale, and he was arrested while doing it by the policemen. And as they were eager to find out about the theft of the jewels from Bite's daughter, they took the prince at once to the chief of police. And when he saw that the culprit was dressed like a hermit, he asked him very gently: "Holy sir, where did you get this pearl necklace? It belongs to Bite's daughter and was stolen." Then the prince said to them: "Gentlemen, my teacher gave it to me to sell. You had better go and ask him."

Then the chief of police went and asked him: "Holy sir, how did this pearl necklace come into your pupil's hand?"

And the shrewd counsellor's son whispered to him: "Sir, as I am a hermit, I wander about all the time in this region. And as I happened to be here in this cemetery, I saw a whole company of witches who came here at night. And one of the witches split open the heart of a king's son, and offered it to her master. She was mad with wine, and screwed up her face most horribly. But when she impudently tried to snatch my rosary as I prayed, I became angry, and branded her on the hip with a three-pronged fork which I had made red-hot with a magic spell. And I took this pearl necklace from her neck. Then, as it was not a thing for a hermit, I sent it to be sold."

When he heard this, the chief of police went and told the whole story to the king. And when the king heard and saw the evidence, he sent the old woman, who was reliable, to identify the pearl necklace. And he heard from her that Lily was branded on the hip.

Then he was convinced that she was really a witch and had devoured his son. So he went himself to the counsellor's son, who was disguised as a hermit, and asked how Lily should be punished. And by his advice, she was banished from the city, though her parents wept. So she was banished naked to the forest and knew that the counsellor's son had done it all, but she did not die.

And at nightfall the prince and the counsellor's son put off their hermit disguise, mounted on horseback, and found her weeping. They put her on a horse and took her to their own country. And when they got there, the prince lived most happily with her.

But Bite thought that his daughter was eaten by wild beasts in the wood, and he died of grief. And his wife died with him.

When he had told this story, the goblin asked the king: "O King, who was to blame for the death of the parents: the prince, or the counsellor's son, or Lily? You seem like a very wise man, so resolve my doubts on this point. If you know and do not tell me the truth, then your head will surely fly into a hundred pieces. And if you give a good answer, then I will jump from your shoulder and go back to the sissoo tree."

Then King Triple-victory said to the goblin: "You are a master of magic. You surely know yourself, but I will tell you. It was not the fault of any of the three you mentioned. It was entirely the fault of King Ear-lotus."

But the goblin said: "How could it be the king's fault? The other three did it. Are the crows to blame when the geese eat up the rice?"

Then the king said: "But those three are not to blame. It was right for the counsellor's son to do his master's business. So he is not to blame. And Lily and the prince were madly in love and could not stop to think. They only looked after their own affairs. They are not to blame.

"But the king knew the law-books very well, and he had spies to find out the facts among the people. And he knew about the doings of rascals. So he acted without thinking. He is to blame."

When the goblin heard this, he wanted to test the king's constancy. So he went back by magic in a moment to the sissoo tree. And the king went back fearlessly to get him.

The Three Lovers who brought the Dead Girl to Life
Whose wife should she be?

Then King Triple-victory went back under the sissoo tree to fetch the goblin. And when he got there and looked about, he saw the goblin fallen on the ground and moaning. Then, when the king put the body with the goblin in it on his shoulder and started to carry him off quickly and silently, the goblin on his shoulder said to him: "Oh King, you have fallen into a very disagreeable task which you do not deserve. So to amuse you I will tell another story. Listen."

On the bank of Kalindi River is a farm where a very learned Brahman lived. And he had a very beautiful daughter named Coral. When the Creator fashioned her fresh and peerless loveliness, surely he must have despised the cleverness he showed before in fashioning the nymphs of heaven.

When she had grown out of childhood, there came from the city of Kanauj three Brahman youths, endowed with all the virtues. And each of them asked her father for her, that she might be his own. And though her father would rather have died than give her up to anyone, he made up his mind to give her to one of them. But the girl would not marry any one of them for some time, because she was afraid of hurting the feelings of the other two. So they stayed there all three of them day and night, feasting on the beauty of her face, like the birds that live on moonbeams.

Then all at once Coral fell sick of a burning fever and died. And when the Brahman youths saw that she was dead, they were smitten with grief. But they adorned her body, took it to the cemetery, and burned it.

And one of them built a hut there, slept on a bed made of her ashes, and got his food by begging. The second took her bones and went to dip them in the sacred Ganges river. And the third became a monk and wandered in other countries.

And as he wandered, the monk came to a village called Thunderbolt, and was entertained in the house of a Brahman. But when he had been honoured by the master of the house and had begun to eat dinner there, the little boy began to cry and would not stop even when they petted him. So his mother took him on her arm, and angrily threw him into the blazing fire. And being tender, he was reduced to ashes in a moment.

When the monk saw this, his hair stood on end, and he said: "Alas! I have come into the house of a devil. I will not eat this food. It would be like eating sin." But the master of the house said to him: "Brahman, I have studied to good purpose. See my skill in bringing the dead to life." So he opened a book, took out a magic spell, read it, and sprinkled water on the ashes. And the moment the water was sprinkled, the boy stood up alive just as before. Then the monk was highly delighted and finished his dinner with pleasure.

And the master of the house hung the book on an ivory peg, took dinner with the monk, and went to bed. When he was asleep, the monk got up quietly, and tremblingly took the book, hoping to bring his darling Coral back to life. He went away and travelled night and day, until he finally reached the cemetery. And he caught sight of the second youth, who had come back after dipping the bones in the Ganges. And he also found the third youth, who had made a hut and lived there, sleeping on the girl's ashes.

Then the monk cried: "Brother, leave your hut. I will bring the dear girl back to life." And while they eagerly questioned him, he opened the book, and read the magic spell, and sprinkled holy water on the ashes. And Coral immediately stood up, alive. And the girl was more beautiful than ever. She looked as if she were made of gold.

When the three youths saw her come back to life like that, they went mad with love, and fought with one another to possess her.

One said: "I brought her to life by my magic spell. She is my wife."

The second said: "She came to life because of my journey to the sacred river. She is my wife."

The third said: "I kept her ashes. That is why she came to life. She is my dear wife."

O King, you are able to decide their dispute. Tell me. Whose wife should she be? If you know and say what is false, then your head will split.

When the king heard this, he said to the goblin: "The man who painfully found the magic spell and brought her back to life, he did only what a father ought to do. He is not her husband. And the man who went to dip her bones in the sacred river, he did only what a son ought to do. He is not her husband. But the man who slept with her ashes and lived a hard life in the cemetery, he did what a lover ought to do. He deserves to be her husband."

When the goblin heard this answer of King Triple-victory, he suddenly escaped from his shoulder and went back. And the king wished to do as the monk had asked him; so he decided to go back and get him. Great-minded people do not waver until they have kept their promises, even at the cost of life.

The Parrot and the Thrush
Which are worse, men or women?

Then the king went back to the sissoo tree to fetch the goblin. When he got there, he took the body with the goblin in it on his shoulder, and started off in silence. And as he walked along, the goblin said to him again: "O King, you must be very tired, coming and going in the night. So to amuse you I will tell another story. Listen."

There is a city called Patna, the gem of the earth. And long ago a king lived there whose name was Lion-of-Victory. Fate had made him the owner of all virtues and all wealth. And he had a parrot called Jewel-of-Wisdom, that had divine intelligence and knew all the sciences, but lived as a parrot because of a curse.

This king had a son called Moon, and by the advice of the parrot this prince married the daughter of the king of the Magadha country; and her name was Moonlight. Now this princess had a thrush named Moony, who was like the parrot, because she had learning and intelligence. And the parrot and the thrush lived in one cage in the palace.

One day the parrot eagerly said to the thrush: "My darling, love me, and share my bed and my chair and my food and my amusements."

But the thrush said: "I will have nothing to do with men. Men are bad and ungrateful."

Then the parrot said: "Men are not bad. It is only women who are bad and cruel-hearted." And they quarrelled.

Then the two birds wagered their freedom with each other and went to the prince to have their quarrel decided. And the prince mounted his father's judgment throne, and when he had heard the cause of the quarrel, he asked the thrush: "How are men ungrateful? Tell the truth." Then she said, "Listen, O Prince," and to prove her point she started to tell this story illustrating the faults of men.

There is a famous city called Kamandaki, where a wealthy merchant lived named Fortune. And in time a son was born to him and named Treasure. Then when the father went to heaven, the young man became very unruly because of gambling and other vices. And the rascals came together, and ruined him. Association with scoundrels is the root from which springs the tree of calamity.

So in no long time he lost all he had through his vices, and being ashamed of his poverty, he left his own country and went to wander in other places. And during his travels he came to a city called Sandal City, and entered the house of a merchant, seeking something to eat. When the merchant saw the youth, he asked him about his family, and finding that he was a gentleman, he entertained him. And thinking that Gate had sent the young man, he gave him his own daughter Pearl, together with some money. And when Treasure was married, he lived in his father-in-law's house.

As time passed, he forgot his former miseries in the comforts of his life, and longed for the old vices, and wanted to go home. So the rascal managed to persuade his father-in-law, who had no other children, took his wife Pearl with her beautiful ornaments, and an old woman, and started for his own country. Presently he came to a wood where he said he was afraid of thieves, so he took all his wife's ornaments. Perceive, O Prince, how cruel and hard are the ungrateful hearts of those who indulge in gambling and other vices. And the scoundrel was ready, just for money, to kill his good wife. He threw her and the old woman into a pit. Then the rascal went away and the old woman perished there.

But Pearl, with the little life she had left, managed to get out by clinging to the grass and bushes, and weeping bitterly, and bleeding, she asked the way step by step, and painfully reached her father's house by the way she had come. And her mother and father were surprised and asked her: "Why did you come back so soon, and in this condition?"

And that good wife said: "On the road we were robbed, and my husband was forcibly carried off. And the old woman fell into a pit and died, but I escaped. And a kind-hearted traveller pulled me from the pit." Then her father and mother were saddened, but they comforted her, and Pearl stayed there, true to her husband.

Then in time Treasure lost all his money in gambling, and he reflected: "I will get more money from the house of my father-in-law. I will go there and tell my father-in-law that his daughter is well and is at my house."

So he went again to his father-in-law. And as he went, his ever-faithful wife saw him afar off. She ran and fell at the rascal's feet and told him all the story that she had invented for her parents. For the heart of a faithful wife does not change even when she learns that her husband is a rogue.

Then that rascal went without fear into the house of his father-in-law and bowed low before his feet. And his father-in-law rejoiced when he saw him and made a great feast with his relatives, for he said: "My son is delivered alive from the robbers. Heaven be praised!" Then Treasure enjoyed the wealth of his father-in-law and lived with his wife Pearl.

Now one night this worst of scoundrels did what I ought not to repeat, but I will tell it, or my story would be spoiled. Listen, O Prince. While Pearl lay asleep trusting him, that wretch killed her in the night, stole all her jewels, and escaped to his own country. This shows how bad and ungrateful men are.

When the thrush had told her story, the prince smiled and said to the parrot: "It is your turn now."

Then the parrot said: "Your Majesty, women are cruel and reckless and bad. To prove it, I will tell you a story. Listen."

There is a city called Joyful, where lived a prince of merchants named Virtue, who owned millions of money. He had a daughter named Fortune, peerless in beauty, dearer to him than life. And she was given in marriage to a merchant's son from Copper City, whose name was Ocean. He was her equal in wealth, beauty, and family; a delight to the eyes of men.

One day when her husband was away from home, she saw from the window a handsome young man. And the moment she saw him, the fickle girl went mad with love, and secretly sent a messenger to invite him in, and made love to him in secret. Thus her heart was fixed on him alone, and she was happy with him.

But at last her husband came home and delighted the hearts of his parents-in-law. And when the day had been spent in feasting, Fortune was adorned by her mother, and sent to her husband's room. But she was cold toward him and pretended to sleep. And her husband went to sleep, too, for he was weary with his journey, and had been drinking wine.

When everyone in the house had gone to sleep after their dinner, a thief made a hole in the wall and came into that very room. And just then the merchant's daughter got up without seeing him, and went out secretly to a meeting with her lover. And the thief was disappointed, and thought: "She has gone out into the night wearing the very jewels that I came to steal. I must see where she goes." So the thief went out and followed her.

But she met a woman friend who had flowers in her hand, and went to a park not very far away. And there she saw the man whom she came to meet hanging on a tree. For the policeman had thought he was a thief, had put a rope around his neck and hanged him.

And at the sight she went distracted, and lamented pitifully: "Oh, oh! I am undone," and fell on the ground and wept. Then she took her lover down from the tree and made him sit up, though he was dead, and adorned him with perfumes and jewels and flowers.

But when in her love-madness she lifted his face and kissed him, a goblin who had come to live in her dead lover, bit off her nose. And she was startled and ran in pain from the spot. But then she came back to see if perhaps he was alive after all. But the goblin had gone, and she saw that he was motionless and dead. So she slowly went back home, frightened and disgraced and weeping.

And the concealed thief saw it all and thought: "What has the wicked woman done? Alas! Can women be so dreadful as this? What might she not do next?" So out of curiosity the thief still followed her from afar.

And the wretched woman entered the house and cried aloud, and said: "Save me from my cruel enemy, my own husband. He cut off my nose and I had done nothing." And her servants heard her cries and all arose in excitement. Her husband too awoke. Then her father came and saw that her nose was cut off, and in his anger he had his son-in-law arrested.

And the poor man did not know what to do. Even when he was being bound, he remained silent and said nothing. Then they all woke up and heard the story, but the thief who knew the whole truth, ran away. And when day came, the merchant's son was haled before the king by his father-in-law. And Fortune went there without her nose, and the king heard the whole story and condemned the merchant's son to death for mistreating his wife.

So the innocent, bewildered man was led to the place of execution and the drums were beaten. Just then the thief came up and said to the king's men: "Why do you kill this man without any good reason? I know how the whole thing happened. Take me to the king, and I will tell all."

So all the king's men took him to the king. And the thief told the king all the adventures of the night, and said: "Your Majesty, if you cannot trust my word, you may find the nose at this moment between the teeth of the dead body."

Then the king sent men to investigate, and when he found it was true, he released the merchant's son from the punishment of death. As for wretched Fortune, he cut off her ears, too, and banished her from the country. And he took from her father, the merchant, all his money, and made the thief the chief of police. He was pleased with him.

O Prince, this shows how cruel and false women are by nature.

As he spoke these words, the parrot changed into a god, for the curse was fulfilled, and went to heaven like a god. And the thrush suddenly became a goddess, for her curse was at an end, and flew up likewise to heaven. So their dispute was never settled at that court.

When the goblin had told this story, he asked the king: "O King, tell me. Are men bad, or women? If you know and do not tell, your head will fly to pieces." And when the king heard these words of the goblin on his shoulder, he said to that magic goblin: "O goblin! Here and there, now and then, there is an occasional bad man like that. But women are usually bad. We hear about many of them."

Then the goblin disappeared from the king's shoulder as before. And the king tried again to catch him.

King Shudraka and Hero's Family
Which of the five deserves the most honour?

Then King Triple-victory went back under the sissoo tree and caught the goblin, who gave a horse-laugh. But the king without fear put him on his shoulder as before and started toward the monk. And as he walked along, the goblin on his shoulder said to him again: "O King, why do you take such pains for that wretched monk? Have you no sense about this fruitless task? Well, after all, I like your devotion. So, to amuse the weary journey, I will tell you another story. Listen."

There is a city called Beautiful, and it deserves the name. There lived a king named Shudraka, of tremendous power and mighty courage. He was so used to victory that the fire of his courage was kept blazing by the wind from the fans in the hands of the wives of his vanquished foes. Under his rule the earth was rich and always good, as in the days of old. And he was fond of brave men.

Now one day a Brahman named Hero came from Malwa to pay his homage to this king. He had a wife named Virtue, a son named Trusty, and a daughter named Heroic. And he had just three servants, a dagger at his hip, a sword in his hand, and a shield in his other hand. These were all the servants he had when he asked the king for five hundred gold-pieces a day as his wages.

And the king thought from his appearance that he was a remarkably brave man, so he gave him the wages he asked. But out of curiosity he put spies on his track, to learn what he did with all the money.

Now Hero called on the king in the morning, and at noon he took his sword and stood at the palace gate and divided his daily salary. One hundred gold-pieces he gave to his wife for food and household expenses. And with another hundred he bought clothes and perfumes and nuts and such things. And another hundred he devoted to the worship of Vishnu and

Shiva, after taking the ceremonial bath. And the two hundred which were left he gave to Brahmans and the unhappy and the poor. This was the way he divided and spent the money every day. Then after he had sacrificed and eaten dinner, he stood every night alone at the palace gate with his sword and shield. All this King Shudraka learned from his spies and was greatly pleased and forbad the spies to follow him again. For he thought him a wonderful man, worthy of especial honour.

Then one day a veil of clouds covered the sky and poured down rain in streams day and night, so that the highway was quite deserted. Only Hero was at his post as usual by the palace gate. And when the sun set and dreadful darkness was spread abroad and the rain fell in sheets, the king wished to test Hero's behaviour. So at night he climbed to the palace roof and cried: "Who is there at the gate?" And Hero answered: "I am here." And the king thought: "How steadfast this man Hero is, and how devoted to me! I must surely give him a greater post." And he descended from the roof and entered the palace and went to bed.

The next night it rained again in sheets and the world was wrapped in the darkness of death. And again the king thought to test his behaviour, and climbing to the roof he called out toward the palace gate: "Who is there?" And when Hero said: "I am here, your Majesty," the king was greatly astonished.

Just then he heard at a distance a sweet-voiced woman crying. And he thought: "Who is this who laments so piteously, as if in deep despair? In my kingdom there is no violence, no poor man and none distressed. Who can she be?" And being merciful, he called to Hero, who stood below: "Listen, Hero. A woman is weeping at some distance. Go and learn why she weeps and who she is." And Hero said "Certainly," arranged his dagger, took his sword in his hand, and started. He did not even think of the pelting hail, the flashing lightning, or the rain and darkness. And when the king saw him setting out alone in a night like that, he was filled with pity and curiosity, and descending from the palace roof, took his sword and followed all alone, without being seen.

As Hero traced the sound of crying, he came to a beautiful lake outside the city, and there he saw a woman in the midst of the water, lamenting in these words: "Alas for you, brave and merciful and generous! How shall I live without you?"

And Hero was amazed, and timidly asked her: "Who are you, and why do you weep?" And she replied: "O Hero, I am the Goddess of the Earth, and now my lord, this virtuous King Shudraka, is going to die in three days. How shall I find another such master? So I am distracted with grief, and I lament."

When Hero heard this, he was frightened and said: "Goddess, is there any remedy for this, any way in which the king might be saved?" And the goddess answered: "There is just one remedy, my son, and it is in your hands." And Hero said: "Goddess, tell me quickly, that I may adopt it at once. What good would life be to us otherwise?"

Then the goddess said: "My son, there is no other man devoted to his master as you are: so you may learn how to save him. There is a temple to the Dreadful Goddess built by that king near his palace. If you sacrifice your son to her at once, then the king will not die. He will live another hundred years. If you do it this very night, then the blessing will come, not otherwise."

And Hero, the hero, replied: "Then I will go, Goddess, and do it this moment." And the Goddess of the Earth said: "Good fortune go with you," and she vanished. And the king, who had followed secretly, heard it all. So he still followed to find out how Hero would behave.

But Hero went straight home, woke his wife Virtue, and told her all that the Goddess of the Earth had said. And his wife said: "My dear, if so much depends on it, wake the boy and tell him." Then Hero woke the little boy, told him all, and said: "My boy, if you are sacrificed to the Dreadful Goddess, our king will live. If not, he will die in three days."

And the boy was true to his name. Without fear and without hesitation he said: "My dear father, I am a lucky boy if the king lives at the cost of my life. Besides, that would pay for the food we have eaten. Why then delay? Take me quickly and sacrifice me to the goddess. May the king's evil fate be averted by my death!" And Hero was delighted and congratulated him, saying: "Well said! You are indeed my son."

So Hero's wife Virtue and his daughter Heroic went through the night with Hero and Trusty to the temple of the Dreadful Goddess. The king too followed them, disguised and unnoticed. Then the father took Trusty from his shoulder in the presence of the goddess. And Trusty worshipped the goddess, and bravely saluted her, and said: "O Goddess, by the sacrifice of my head may the king live another hundred years and rule a thornless kingdom."

And as he prayed, Hero cut off his head and offered it to the Dreadful Goddess, saying: "May the king live at the cost of my son's life!" Then a voice cried from heaven: "O Hero, who else is devoted to his master as you are? You have given life and royal power to the king at the cost of your only son, and such a son." All this the king himself saw and heard.

Then Hero's daughter Heroic kissed the lips of her dead brother, and was blinded with sorrow, and her heart broke, and she died.

Then Hero's wife Virtue said: "My dear, we have done our duty by the king. And you see how my daughter died of grief. So now I say: What good is life to me without my children? I was a fool before. I should have given my own head to save the king. So now permit me to burn myself at once."

And when she insisted, Hero said: "Do so. What happiness is there in a life of constant mourning for your children? And as for your giving your own life instead, do not grieve about that. If there had been any other way, I should of course have given my life. So wait a moment. I will build you a funeral pile out of these logs." So he built the pile and lighted it.

And Virtue fell at her husband's feet, then worshipped the Dreadful Goddess, and prayed: "O Goddess, may I have the same husband in another life, and may this same King

Shudraka be saved at the cost of my son's life." And she died in the blazing fire.

Then Hero thought: "I have done my duty by the king, as the heavenly voice admitted. And I have paid for the king's food which I have eaten. So now why should I want to live alone? It is not right for a man like me to go on living at the expense of all the family which I ought to support. Why should I not please the goddess by sacrificing myself?"

So Hero first approached the goddess with a hymn of praise: "O Demon-slayer! Saviour! Devil-killer! Trident-holder! Joy of the wise! Protectress of the universe! Victory to thee, O best of mothers, whose feet the world adores! O fearless refuge of the pious! Kali of the dreadful ornaments! Honour and glory to thee, O kindly goddess! Be pleased to accept the sacrifice of my head in behalf of King Shudraka." Then he suddenly cut off his own head with his dagger.

King Shudraka beheld this from his hiding-place, and was filled with amazement and grief and admiration. And he thought: "I have never seen or heard the like of this. That good man and his family have done a hard thing for me. In this strange world who else is so brave as that, to give his son, his family, and his life for his king: If I should not make a full return for his kindness, my kingdom would mean nothing to me, and my life would be the life of a beast. If I lost my virtue, it would all be a disgrace to me."

But when he started to cut off his own head, there came a voice from heaven: "My son, do nothing rash. I am well pleased with your character. The Brahman Hero and his children and his wife shall come back to life." And when the voice ceased, Hero stood up alive and uninjured with his son and his daughter and his wife. Then the king hid himself again and looked on with eyes filled with tears of joy, and could not see enough of them.

Now Hero, like a man awaking from a dream, gazed at his son and his wife and his daughter, and was greatly perplexed. He spoke to each by name, and asked them how they had come to life after being reduced to ashes. "Is this a fancy of mine? Or a dream? Or an illusion? Or the favour of the goddess?" And his wife and children said to him: "By the favour of the goddess we are alive."

At last Hero believed it, and having worshipped the goddess, he went home happy with his children and his wife. And when he had seen his son and his wife and daughter safe at home, he went back that same night to the palace gate.

And King Shudraka saw all this and went back without being seen himself, and climbed to the roof, and called: "Who is there at the gate?" And Hero replied: "Your Majesty, I, Hero, am here. At your command I followed the woman who cried. She must have been a witch, for she vanished the moment I saw her and spoke to her."

When the king heard this, he was astonished beyond measure, for he had seen what really happened. And he thought: "Ah, the hearts of brave men are deep as the sea, if they do not boast after doing an unparalleled action." So the king descended from the roof, entered the palace, and passed the rest of the night there.

Then when the court was held in the morning, Hero came to see the king. And as he stood there, the delighted king told all his counsellors and the others the story of the night. And all were amazed and confounded at hearing of Hero's virtues, and they praised him, crying: "Well done! Well done!"

Then the king and Hero lived happily together, sharing the power equally.

When the goblin had told this story, he asked King Triple-victory: "O King, which of all these was the most worthy? If you know and will not tell, then the curse I told you of will be fulfilled."

And the king said to the goblin: "O magic creature, King Shudraka was the most noble of them all."

But the goblin said: "Why not Hero, the like of whom as a servant is not to be found in the whole world? Or why should not his wife receive the most praise, who did not waver when she saw her son killed like a beast before her eyes? Or why is not the boy Trusty the most worthy, who showed such wonderful manhood when only a little boy? Why do you say that King Shudraka was the best among them?"

Then the king answered the goblin: "Not Hero. He was a gentleman born, so it was his duty to save his king at the cost of life, wife and children. And his wife was a lady, a faithful wife who only did what was right in following her husband. And Trusty was their son, and like them. For the cloth is always like the threads. But the king has aright to use his subjects' lives to save his own. So when Shudraka gave his life for them, he proved himself the best of all."

When the goblin heard this, he jumped from the king's shoulder and went back to his home without being seen. And the king was not disturbed by this magic, but started back through the night to catch him.

The Brave Man, the Wise Man, and the Clever Man
To which should the girl be given?

Then King Triple-victory went back to the sissoo tree and saw the body with the goblin in it hanging there just as before. He took it down without being frightened by all its twistings and writhings, and quickly set out again. And as he walked along in silence as before, the goblin said: "O King, you are obstinate, and you are pleasing to look at. So to amuse you, I will tell another story. Listen."

There is a city called Ujjain, famous throughout the world. There lived a king named Merit, who had as counsellor a Brahman named Hariswami, adorned with all noble virtues. The counsellor had a worthy wife, and a son named Devaswami was born to her, and was as good as she. And they had one daughter named Moonlight, who was worthy of her name, for she was famous for her matchless beauty and charm.

When the girl had grown out of childhood, she was proud of her wonderful beauty, and she told her mother, her father, and her brother: "I will marry a brave man or a wise man or a clever man. I should die if I were married to anyone else."

Now while her father was busy looking for such a husband for her, he was sent by King Merit to another king in the southern country to make a treaty for war and peace. When he had finished his business, a Brahman youth, who had heard of his daughter's beauty, came and asked him for her.

And he said: "My daughter will not marry anyone unless he is a clever man or a wise man or a brave man. Which of these are you? Tell me." And the Brahman said: "I am a clever man." "Show me," said the father, and the clever man made a flying chariot by his skill. Then he took Hariswami in this magic chariot, and carried him to the sky. And he took the delighted father to the camp of the king of the southern country where he had been on business. Then Hariswami appointed the marriage for the seventh day.

At this time another Brahman youth in Ujjain came to the girl's brother and asked him for her. And when he was told that she would marry only a wise man or a clever man or a brave man, he said he was a brave man. Then when he had shown his skill with weapons, the brother promised his sister to the brave man. And without telling his mother, he consulted the star-gazers and appointed the marriage for the seventh day.

At the same time a third Brahman youth came to the girl's mother and asked for the girl. And the mother said: "My son, a wise man or a clever man or a brave man shall marry my daughter but no one else. Which of these are you? Tell me." And he said: "I am a wise man." So she asked him about the past and the future, and found that he was a wise man. Then she promised to give him her daughter on the seventh day.

The next day Hariswami came home and told his wife and his son all that he had done. And she and he each told him all that she or he had done. So Hariswami was greatly perplexed, because three bridegrooms had been invited. Then the seventh day came and the three bridegrooms came to Hariswami's house.

Strange to say, at that moment Moonlight disappeared. Then the wise man said: "A giant named Smoke-tail has carried her to his den in the Vindhya forest."

When Hariswami heard this from the wise man, he was frightened and asked the clever man to find a remedy for the trouble. And the clever man made a chariot as before, full of all kinds of weapons, and brought Hariswami with the wise man and the brave man in a moment to the Vindhya forest. And the wise man showed them the giant's den.

When the giant saw what had happened, he came out in anger, and the brave man fought with him. Then came a famous duel with strange weapons between a man and a giant for the sake of a woman, like the ancient fight between Rama and Ravana. Though the giant was a terrible fighter, the brave man presently cut off his head with an arrow shaped like a half-moon. When the giant was killed, they found Moonlight in the den and all went back to Ujjain in the clever man's chariot.

Then when the proper time for wedding came, there arose a great dispute among the three in Hariswami's house.

The wise man said: "If I had not discovered her by my wisdom, how could you have found her hiding-place? She should be given to me."

The clever man said: "If I had not made a flying chariot, how could you have gone there in a moment and come back like the gods, or how could you have had a chariot-fight with him? She should be given to me."

The brave man said: "If I had not killed the giant in the fight, who would have saved her in spite of all your pains? The girl should be given to me."

And as they quarrelled, Hariswami stood silent, confused, and perplexed.

When the goblin had told this story, he said to the king: "O King, do you say to which of them she should be given. If you know and will not tell, then your head will split into a hundred pieces."

Then the king broke silence and said: "She should be given to the brave man, who risked his life and killed the giant and saved the girl. The wise man and the clever man were only helpers whom Fate gave him. A star-gazer and a chariot-maker work for other people, do they not?"

When the goblin heard this answer, he suddenly escaped from the king's shoulder and went back. And the king determined to get him, and went again to the sissoo tree.

The Girl who transposed the Heads of her Husband and Brother
Which combination of head and body is her husband?

Then the king went back to the sissoo tree, put the goblin on his shoulder as before, and started in silence toward the monk. And the goblin said to him: "O King, you are wise and good, so I am pleased with you. To amuse you, therefore, I will tell you another story with a puzzle in it. Listen."

Long ago there was a king named Glory-banner in the world. His city was named Beautiful. And in this city was a splendid temple to the goddess Gauri. And to the right of the temple was a lake called Bath of Gauri. And on a certain day in each year a great crowd of people came there on a pilgrimage from all directions to bathe.

One day a laundryman named White came there from another village to bathe. And the youth saw a maiden who had also come there to bathe. Her name was Lovely, and her father's name was Clean-cloth. She robbed the moon of its beauty and White of his heart. So he inquired about her name and family and went home lovesick.

When he got there, he was ill and could not eat without her. And when his mother asked him, he told her what was in his heart, but did not change his habits. But she went and told her husband, whose name was Spotless.

So Spotless went and saw how his son was acting, and said: "My son, why should you be downcast? Your desire is not hard to obtain. For if I ask Clean-cloth, he will surely give you his daughter. We are not inferior to him in birth, wealth, or social position. I know him and he knows me. So there is no difficulty about it." Thus Spotless comforted his son, made him eat and take care of himself, went with him the next day to Clean-cloth's house, and asked that the girl might be given to his son White. And Clean-cloth graciously promised to give her to him.

Then when the time came, Clean-cloth gave White his charming daughter, a wife worthy of him. And when he was married, White went happily to his father's house with his sweet bride.

Now as he lived there happily, Lovely's brother came to visit. And when they had all asked him about his health and his sister had greeted him with a kiss, and after he had rested, he said: "My father sent me to invite Lovely and White to a festival in our house." And all the relatives said it was a good plan and entertained him that day with appropriate things to drink and eat.

The next morning White set out for his father-in-law's house, together with his brother-in-law and Lovely. And when he came to the city Beautiful, he saw the great temple of Gauri. And he said to Lovely and her brother: "We will see this goddess. I will go first and you two stay here." So White went in to see the goddess. He entered the temple and bowed before the goddess whose eighteen arms had killed the horrible demons, whose lotus-feet were set upon a giant that she had crushed.

And when he had worshipped her, an idea suddenly came to him. "People honour this goddess with all kinds of living sacrifices. Why should I not win her favour by sacrificing myself?" And he fetched a sword from a deserted inner room, cut off his own head, and let it fall on the floor.

Presently his brother-in-law entered the temple to see why he delayed so long. And when he saw his brother-in-law with his head cut off, he went mad with grief, and cut off his own head in the same way with the same sword.

Then when he failed to come out, Lovely was alarmed and entered the temple. And when she saw her husband and her brother in that condition, she cried: "Alas! This is the end of me!" and fell weeping to the floor. But presently she rose, lamenting for the pair so unexpectantly dead, and thought: "What is my life good for now?"

Before killing herself, she prayed to the goddess: "O Goddess! One only deity of happiness and character! Partaker of the life of Shiva! Refuge of all women-folk! Destroyer of

grief! Why have you killed my husband and my brother at
one fell swoop? It was not right, for I was always devoted to
you. Then be my refuge when I pray to you, and hear my one
pitiful prayer. I shall leave this wretched body of mine on this
spot, but in every future life of mine, O Goddess, may I have
the same husband and brother." Thus she prayed, praised,
and worshipped the goddess, then tied a rope to an ashoka
tree which grew there.

But while she was arranging the rope about her neck, a
voice from heaven cried: "Do nothing rash, my daughter.
Leave the rope alone. Though you are young, I am pleased
with your unusual goodness. Place the two heads on the two
bodies and they shall rise up again and live through my
favour."

So Lovely left the rope alone and joyfully went to the
bodies. But in her great hurry and confusion she made a
mistake. She put her husband's head on her brother's body
and her brother's head on her husband's body. Then they
arose, sound and well, like men awaking from a dream. And
they were all delighted to hear one another's adventures,
worshipped the goddess, and went on their way.

Now as she walked along, Lovely noticed that she had
made a mistake in their heads. And she was troubled and did
not know what to do.

When the goblin had told this story, he asked the king: "O
King, when they were mingled in this way, which should be
her husband? If you know and do not tell, then the curse I
spoke of will be fulfilled."

And the king said to the goblin: "The body with the
husband's head on it is her husband. For the head is the most
important member. It is by the head that we recognize
people."

Then the goblin slipped from the king's shoulder as before,
and quickly disappeared. And the king went back,
determined to catch him.

The Mutual Services of King Fierce-lion and Prince Good

Which is the more deserving?

Then the king went back to the sissoo tree, put the goblin on his shoulder as before, and started. And as he walked along, the goblin said: "O King, I will tell you a story to amuse your weariness. Listen."

On the shore of the Eastern Ocean is Copper City. There a king named Fierce-lion lived. He turned his back to other men's wives, but not to fighting men. He destroyed his enemies, but not other men's wealth.

One day a popular prince named Good came from the south to the king's gate. He introduced himself, but did not get what he wanted from the king. And he thought: "If I am born a prince, why am I so poor? And if I am to be poor, why did God give me so many desires? For this king pays no attention to me, though I wait upon him and grow weary and faint with hunger."

While he was thinking, the king went hunting. He went with many horsemen and footmen, and the prince ran along in the dress of a pilgrim with a club in his hand. And during the hunt the king chased a great boar a long distance, and so came into another forest. There he lost sight of the boar, for the trail was covered with leaves and grass. And the king was tired and lost his way in the forest. Only the pilgrim-prince thought nothing of his life, and hungry and thirsty as he was, he followed on foot the king who rode a swift horse.

And when the king saw him following, he spoke lovingly: "My good man, do you perhaps know the way we came?"

And the pilgrim bowed low and said: "I know, your Majesty. But first rest yourself a moment. The blazing sun, the middle jewel in the girdle of heaven's bride, is terribly hot." Then the king said eagerly: "See if there is water anywhere."

And the pilgrim agreed and climbed a high tree and looked around. And he saw a river and climbed down and took the king to it. He unsaddled the horse, gave him water and grass, and let him rest. And when the king had bathed, the pilgrim took two fine mangoes from his skirt, washed them and gave them to the king.

"Where did you get these?" asked the king, and the pilgrim bowed and said: "Your Majesty, I have lived on such food for ten years. While I was serving your Majesty, I had to live like a monk." And the king said: "What can I say? You deserve your name of Good." And he was filled with pity and shame, and thought: "A curse on kings, who do not know whether their servants are happy or not! And a curse of their attendants, who do not tell them this and that!" And when the pilgrim insisted, the king was prevailed on to take the two mangoes. He rested there with the pilgrim and ate the mangoes and drank water with the pilgrim, who was accustomed to eat mangoes and drink water.

Then the pilgrim saddled the horse and went ahead to show the way, and at last, at the king's command, mounted behind on the horse; so the king found his soldiers and went safely home. And when he got there, he proclaimed the devotion of the pilgrim, and made him a rich man, but could not feel that he had paid his debt. So Good stayed there happily with King Fierce-lion and stopped living as a pilgrim.

One day the king sent Good to Ceylon to ask for the hand of the daughter of the King of Ceylon. So he set out after sacrificing to the proper god, and entered a ship with some Brahmans chosen by the king. And when the ship had safely reached the middle of the ocean, there suddenly arose from the waves a very large flag-pole made of gold, with a top that touched the sky. It was adorned with waving banners of various colours and was quite astonishing.

At the same moment the clouds gathered, it began to rain violently, and a mighty wind blew. And the ship was driven by the storm winds and caught on the flag-pole. Then the pole began to sink, dragging the ship with it into the raging waves. And the Brahmans who were there were overcome with fear and cursed the name of their king Fierce-lion.

But Good could not endure that because of his devotion to his king. He took his sword in his hand, girt up his garment, and threw himself after the flag-pole into the sea. He had no fear of the pole which seemed a refuge from the ocean. Then as he sank, the ship was battered by the winds and waves and broke up. And all in it fell into the mouths of sharks.

But Good sank into the ocean, and when he looked about he saw a wonderful city. There he entered a shrine to Gauri, tall as the heavenly mountain, with great gem-sprinkled banners on walls made of different kinds of jewels, in a golden temple blazing with jewelled pillars, with a garden that had a pool, the stairs to which were made of splendid gems. After he had bowed low and praised and worshipped the goddess there, he sat down before her in amazement, wondering if it was all a conjuror's trick.

Just then the door was suddenly opened by a heavenly maiden. Her eyes were like lotuses, her face like the moon. She had a smile like a flower and a body soft as lotus-stems. And a thousand women waited upon her. She entered the shrine of the goddess and the heart of Good at the same moment. And when she had worshipped the goddess there, she went out from the shrine, but not from the heart of Good.

She entered a circle of light, and Good followed her. And he saw another splendid house, that seemed like a place of meeting for all riches and all enjoyments. And he saw the girl sitting on a jewelled couch, and he approached and sat beside her. He was like a man painted in a picture, for his eyes were fastened on her face.

Now a servant of the maiden saw that his body was thrilled, that he was intent upon the maiden, that he was in love. She understood his feelings and said to him: "Sir, you are our guest. Enjoy the hospitality of my mistress. Arise. Bathe. Eat." And he felt a little hope at her words and went to a pool in the garden which she showed him.

He plunged into the pool, and when he rose to the surface, he found himself in the pool of King Fierce-lion in Copper City. And when he saw that he had come there so suddenly, he thought: "Oh, what does it mean? Where is that heavenly garden? What a difference between the sight of that girl which was like nectar to me, and this immediate separation from her which is like terrible poison! It was no dream. I was awake when the serving-maid deceived me and made a fool of me."

He was like a madman without the girl. He wandered in the garden and mourned in a lovelorn way. He was surrounded by wind-blown flower-pollen which seemed to him the yellow flames of separation. And when the gardener saw him in this state, he went and told the king.

And the king was troubled. He went himself to see Good, and asked him soothingly: "What does this mean? Tell me, my friend. Where did you go? And where did you come? And where did you stay? And what did you fall into?"

Then Good told him the whole adventure. And the king thought: "Ah, it is fortunate for me that this brave man is lovelorn. For now I have a chance to pay my debt to him." So the king said to him: "My friend, give over this vain grief. I will go with you by the same road, and bring you to the heavenly maiden." So he comforted Good, and made him take a bath.

The next day he transferred his royal duties to his counsellors and entered a ship with Good. Good showed the way through the sea and they saw the flag-pole with its banners rising as before in the middle of the ocean. Then Good said to the king: "Your Majesty, here is the magic flag-pole standing up. When I sink down there, you must sink too along the flag-pole." So when they came near the sinking pole, Good jumped first, and the king followed him.

They sank down and came to the heavenly city. And the king was astonished, and after he had worshipped the goddess, he sat down with Good. Then the girl, like Beauty personified, came out of the circle of light with her friends. "There she is, the lovely creature," said Good, and the king thought: "He is quite right to love her." But when she saw the king looking like a god, she wondered who the strange and wonderful man might be, and entered the shrine to worship the goddess.

But the king took Good and went into the garden to show how little he cared about her. A moment later the girl came from the shrine; she had been praying for a good husband. And she said to a girl friend: "My friend, I wonder where I could see the man who was here. Where is the great man? You girls must hunt for him and ask him to be good enough to come and accept our hospitality. For he is a wonderful man, and we must be polite to him."

So the girl found him in the garden and gave him her mistress' message very respectfully. But the brave king spoke loftily to her: "Your words are hospitality enough. Nothing else is necessary."

Now when her mistress had heard what he said, she thought he was a noble character, better than anybody else. She was attracted by the courage of the king in refusing a sort of hospitality which was almost too much to offer a mere man, and thought about the fulfilment of her prayer for a husband. So she went into the garden herself. She drew near to the king and lovingly begged him to accept her hospitality.

But the king pointed to Good and said: "My dear girl, he told me of the goddess here, and I came to see her. And by following the flag-pole I saw the goddess and her very marvellous temple. It was only afterwards that I happened to see you."

Then the girl said: "O King, you may be interested in seeing a city which is the wonder of the three worlds." And the king laughed and said: "He told me about that, too. I believe there is a pool for bathing there." And the girl said: "O King, do not say that. I am not a deceitful girl. Why should I deceive an honourable man, especially as your noble character has made me feel like a servant? Pray do not refuse me."

So the king agreed and went with Good and the girl to the edge of the circle of light. There a door opened and he entered and saw another heavenly city like a second hill of heaven; for it was built of gems and gold, and the flowers and fruits of every season grew there at the same time.

And the princess seated the king on a splendid throne and brought him gifts and said: "Your Majesty, I am the daughter

of the great god Black-wheel. But Vishnu sent my father to
heaven. And I inherited these two magic cities where one has
everything he wants. There is no old age or death to trouble
us here. And now you are in the place of my father to rule
over the cities and over me." So she offered him herself and
all she had. But the king said: "In that case you are my
daughter and I give you in marriage to my brave friend good."

In the king's words she saw the fulfilment of her prayer,
and being sensible and modest, she agreed. So the king
married them and gave all the magic wealth to happy Good,
and said: "My friend, I have paid you now for one of the two
mangoes which I ate. But I remain in your debt for the
second."

Then he asked the princess how he could get back to his
city. And she gave the king a sword called Invincible, and the
magic fruit which wards off birth, old age, and death. And the
king took the sword and the fruit, plunged into the pool which
she showed him, and came up in his own country, feeling
completely successful. But Good ruled happily over the
kingdom of the princess.

When the goblin had told this story, he asked the king: "O
King, which of these two deserves more credit for plunging
into the sea?"

And the king was afraid of the curse, so he gave a true
answer: "Good seems to me the more deserving, for he did not
know the truth beforehand, but plunged without hope into
the sea, while the king knew the truth when he jumped."

And as soon as the king broke silence, the goblin slipped
from his shoulder as before without being seen and went to
the sissoo tree. And the king tried as before to catch him.
Brave men do not waver until they have finished what they
have begun.

The Specialist in Food, the Specialist in Women, and the Specialist in Cotton
Which is the cleverest?

So the king went back under the sissoo tree, caught the goblin just as before, put him on his shoulder, and started toward the monk. And as he walked along, the goblin on his shoulder spoke and said: "O King, listen once more to the following story to beguile your weariness."

In the Anga country there is a great region called Forest. There lived a great Brahman, pious and wealthy, whose name was Vishnu-swami. To his worthy wife three sons were born, one after another. When they had grown to be young men, specialists in matters of luxury, they were sent one day by their father to find a turtle for a sacrifice which he had begun.

So the brothers went to the ocean and there they found a turtle. Then the eldest said to the two younger: "One of you take this turtle for Father's sacrifice. I cannot carry a slimy thing that smells raw."

But when the eldest said this, the two younger said: "Sir, if you feel disgust, why shouldn't we?"

When the eldest heard this, he said: "You take the turtle, otherwise Father's sacrifice will be ruined on your account. Then you and Father too will surely go to hell."

When they heard him, the two younger brothers laughed and said: "Sir, you seem to know our common duty, but not your own."

Then the eldest said: "What? Are you not aware that I am a connoisseur in food? For I am a specialists in foods. How can I touch this loathsome thing?"

When he heard these words, the second brother said: "But I am even more of a connoisseur. I am a specialist in women. So how can I touch it?"

After this speech, the eldest said to the youngest: "Do you then, being younger than we, carry the turtle."

Then the youngest frowned and said to them: "Fools! I am a great specialist in cotton."

So the three brothers quarrelled, and arrogantly leaving the turtle behind them, they went to have the matter decided at Pinnacle, the capital of a king called Conqueror. When they came there, and had been announced and introduced by the door-keeper, they told their story to the king. And when the king had heard all, he said: "Stay here. I will examine you one after another." So they agreed and all stayed there.

Then the king invited them in at his own dinner hour, seated them on magnificent seats, and set before them sweet dishes of six flavours, fit for a king. While all the rest ate, one of the Brahmans, the specialist in food, disgustedly shook his head and refused to eat. And when the king himself asked him why he would not eat food that was sweet and savoury, he respectfully replied: "Your Majesty, in this food there is the odour of smoke from a burning corpse. Therefore, I do not wish to eat it, however sweet it may be."

Then at the king's command all the rest smelt of it and declared it the best of winter rice, and perfectly sweet. But the food-critic held his nose and would not touch it. Now when the king reflected and made a careful investigation, he learned from the commissioners that the dish was made of rice grown near a village crematory. Then he was greatly astonished and pleased, and said: "Brahman, you are certainly a judge of food. Pray take something else."

After dinner the king dismissed them to their rooms, and sent for the most beautiful woman of his court. And at night he sent this lovely creature, all adorned, to the second brother, the specialist in women. She came with a servant of the king to his chamber, and when she entered, she seemed to illuminate the room. But the judge of women almost fainted, and stopping his nose with his left hand, he said to his servants: "Take her away! If not, I shall die. A goaty smell issues from her."

So the servants, in distress and astonishment, conducted her to the king and told him what had happened. Then the king sent for the specialist in women, and said: "Brahman, she has anointed herself with sandal, camphor, and aloes, so that a delightful perfume pervades her neighbourhood. How could this woman have a goaty smell?" But in spite of this the specialist in women would not yield. And when the king endeavoured to learn the truth, he heard from her own lips that in her infancy she had been separated from her mother and had been brought up on goat's milk. Then the king was greatly astonished and loudly praised the critical judgment of the specialist in women.

Quickly he had a couch prepared for the third brother, the specialist in cotton. So the critic of cotton went to sleep on a bed with seven quilts over the frame and covered with a pure, soft coverlet. When only a half of the first watch of the night was gone, he suddenly started from the bed, shouting and writhing with pain, his hand pressed to his side. And the king's men who were stationed there saw the curly red outline of a hair deeply imprinted on his side.

They went at once and informed the king, who said to them: "See whether there is anything under the quilts or not." So they went and searched under each quilt, and under the last they found one hair, which they immediately took and showed to the king. And the king summoned the specialist in cotton, and finding the mark exactly corresponding to the hair, was filled with extreme astonishment. And he spent that night wondering how the hair could sink into his body through seven quilts.

Now when the king arose in the morning, he was delighted with their marvellous critical judgment and sensitiveness, so that he gave each of the three specialists a hundred thousand gold-pieces. And they were contented and stayed there, forgetting all about the turtle, and thus incurring a crime through the failure of their father's sacrifice.

When he had told this remarkable story, the goblin on the king's shoulder said: "O King, remember the curse I spoke of and declare which of these three was the cleverest."

When he heard this, the wise king answered the goblin: "Without doubt I regard the specialist in cotton as the cleverest, on whose body the imprint of the hair was seen to appear visibly. The other two might possibly have found out beforehand."

When the king had said this, the goblin slipped from his shoulder as before. And the king went back under the sissoo tree again to fetch him.

The Four Scientific Suitors.
To which should the girl be given?

Then the king went back to the sissoo tree, put the goblin on his shoulder, and started. And the goblin spoke to him again: "O King, why do you go to such pains in this cemetery at night? Do you not see the home of the ghosts, full of dreadful creatures, terrible in the night, wrapped in darkness as in smoke? Why do you work so hard and grow weary for the sake of that monk? Well, to amuse the journey, listen to a puzzle which I will tell you."

In the Avanti country is a city built by the gods at the beginning of time, adorned with wonderful wealth and opportunities for enjoyment. In the earliest age it was called Lotus City, then Pleasure City, then Golden City, and now it is called Ujjain. There lived a king named Heroic. And his queen was named Lotus.

One day the king went with her to the sacred Ganges river and prayed to Shiva that he might have children. And after long prayer he heard a voice from heaven, for Shiva was at last pleased with his devotion: "O King, there shall be born to you a brave son to continue your dynasty, and a daughter more beautiful than the nymphs of heaven."

When he heard the heavenly voice, the king was delighted at the fulfilment of his wishes, and went back to his city with the queen. And first Queen Lotus bore a son called Brave, and then a daughter named Grace who put the god of love to shame.

When the girl grew up, the king sought for a suitable husband for her, and invited all the neighbouring princes by letter, but not one of them seemed good enough for her. So the king tenderly said to his daughter: "My dear, I do not see a husband worthy of you, so I will summon all the kings hither, and you shall choose." But the princess said: "My dear father, such a choice would be very embarrassing. I would rather not. Just marry me to any good-looking young man, who understands a single science from beginning to end. I wish nothing more nor less than that."

Now while the king was looking for such a husband, four brave, good-looking, scientific men from the south heard of the matter and came to him. And when they had been hospitably received, each explained his own science to the king.

The first said: "I am a working-man, and my name is Five-cloth. I make five splendid suits of clothes a day. One I give to some god and one to a Brahman. One I wear myself, and one I shall give to my wife when I have one. The fifth I sell, to buy food and things. This is my science. Pray give me Grace."

The second said: "I am a farmer, and my name is Linguist. I understand the cries of all beasts and birds. Pray give me the princess."

The third said: "I am a strong-armed soldier, and my name is Swordsman. I have no rival on earth in the science of swordsmanship. O King, pray give me your daughter."

The fourth said: "O King, I am a Brahman, and my name is Life. I possess a wonderful science. For if dead creatures are brought to me, I can quickly restore them to life. Let your daughter find a husband in a man who has such heroic skill."

When they had spoken, and the king had seen that they all had wonderful garments and personal beauty, he and his daughter swung in doubt.

When the goblin had told this story, he said to the king: "Remember the curse I mentioned, and tell me to which of them the girl should be given."

And the king said to the goblin: "Sir, you are merely trying to gain time by making me break silence. There is no puzzle about that. How could a warrior's daughter be given to a working- man, a weaver? Or to a farmer, either? And as to his knowledge of the speech of beasts and birds, of what practical use is it? And what good is a Brahman who neglects his own affairs and turns magician, despising real courage? Of course she should be given to the warrior Swordsman who had some manhood with his science."

When the goblin heard this, he escaped by magic from the king's shoulder, and disappeared. And the king followed him as before. Discouragement never enters the brave heart of a resolute man.

The Three Delicate Wives of King Virtue-banner
Which is the most delicate?

Then the king went to the sissoo tree, put the goblin on his shoulder once more, and started toward the monk. And as he walked along, the goblin on his shoulder said: "O King, I will tell you a strange story to relieve your weariness. Listen."

There once was a king in Ujjain, whose name was Virtue-banner. He had three princesses as wives, and loved them dearly. One of them was named Crescent, the second Star, and the third Moon. While the king lived happily with his wives, he conquered all his enemies, and was content.

One day at the time of the spring festival, the king went to the garden to play with his three wives. There he looked at the flower-laden vines with black rows of bees on them; they seemed like the bow of the god of love, all ready for service. He heard the songs of nightingales in the trees; they sounded like commands of Love. And with his wives he drank wine which seemed like Love's very life-blood.

Then the king playfully pulled the hair of Queen Crescent, and a lotus-petal fell from her hair into her lap. And the queen was so delicate that it wounded her, and she screamed and fainted. And the king was distracted, but when servants sprinkled her with cool water and fanned her, she gradually recovered consciousness. And the king took her to the palace and waited upon his dear wife with a hundred remedies which the physicians brought.

And when the king saw that she was made comfortable for the night, he went to the palace balcony with his second wife Star. Now while she slept on the king's breast, the moonbeams found their way through the window and fell upon her. And she awoke in a moment, and started up, crying "I am burned!" Then the king awoke and anxiously asked what the matter was, and he saw great blisters on her body. When he asked her about it, Queen Star said: "The moonbeams that fell on me did it." And the king was distracted when he saw how she wept and suffered. He called the servants and they made a couch of moist lotus-leaves, and dressed her wounds with damp sandal-paste.

At that moment the third queen, Moon, left her room to go to the king. And as she moved through the noiseless night, she clearly heard in a distant part of the palace the sound of pestles grinding grain. And she cried: "Oh, oh! It will kill me!" She wrung her hands and sat down in agony in the hall. But her servants returned and led her to her room, where she took to her bed and wept. And when the servants asked what the matter was, she tearfully showed her hands with bruises on them, like two lilies with black bees clinging to them. So they went and told the king. And he came in great distress, and asked his dear wife about it. She showed her hands and spoke, though she suffered: "My dear, when I heard the sound of the pestles, these bruises came." Then the king made them give her a cooling plaster of sandal-paste and other things.

And the king thought: "One of them was wounded by a falling lotus-petal. The second was burned by the moonbeams. The third had her hands terribly bruised by the sound of pestles. I love them dearly, but alas! The very delicacy which is so great a virtue, is positively inconvenient."

And he wandered about in the palace, and it seemed as if the night had three hundred hours. But in the morning the king and his skilful physicians took such measures that before long his wives were well and he was happy.

When he had told this story, the goblin asked: "O King, which of them was the most delicate?" And the king said: "The one who was bruised by the mere sound of the pestles, when nothing touched her. The other two who were wounded or blistered by actual contact with lotus-petals or moonbeams, are not equal to her."

When the goblin heard this, he went back, and the king resolutely hastened to catch him again.

ELEVENTH GOBLIN

The King who won a Fairy as his Wife
Why did his counsellor's heart break?

Then the king went as before to the sissoo tree, put the
goblin on his shoulder, and started back. And the goblin said
once more: "O King, I like you wonderfully well because you
are not discouraged. So I will tell you a delightful little story
to relieve your weariness. Listen."

In the Anga country was a young king named Glory-
banner, so beautiful that he seemed an incarnation of the god
of love. He had conquered all his enemies by his strength of
arm, and he had a counsellor named Farsight.

At last the king, proud of his youth and beauty, entrusted
all the power in his quiet kingdom to his counsellor, and
gradually devoted himself entirely to pleasure. He spent all
his time with the ladies of the court, and listened more
attentively to their love-songs than to the advice of
statesmen. He took greater pleasure in peeping into their
windows than into the holes in his administration. But
Farsight bore the whole burden of public business, and never
wearied day or night.

Then the people began to murmur: "The counsellor Farsight
has seduced the king, and now he alone has all the kingly
glory." And the counsellor said to his wife, whose name was
Prudence: "My dear, the king is devoted to his pleasures, and
great infamy is heaped upon me by the people. They say I
have devoured the kingdom, though in fact I support the
burden of it. Now popular gossip damages the greatest man.
Was not Rama forced to abandon his good wife by popular
clamour? So what shall I do now?"

Then his clever wife Prudence showed that she deserved
her name. She said: "My dear, leave the king and go on a
pilgrimage. Tell him that you are an old man now, and
should be permitted to travel in foreign countries for a time.
Then the gossip will cease, when they see that you are
unselfish. And when you are gone, the king will bear his own

burdens. And thus his levity will gradually disappear. And when you come back, you can assume your office without reproach."

To this advice the counsellor assented, and said to the king in the course of conversation: "Your Majesty, permit me to go on a pilgrimage for a few days. Virtue seems of supreme importance to me."

But the king said: "No, no, counsellor. Is there no other kind of virtue except in pilgrimages? How about generosity and that kind of thing? Isn't it possible to prepare for heaven in your own house?"

Then the counsellor said: "Your Majesty, one gets worldly prosperity from generosity and that kind of thing. But a pilgrimage gives eternal life. A prudent man should attend to it while he has strength. The chance may be lost, for no one can be sure of his health."

But the king was still arguing against it when the doorkeeper came in and said: "Your Majesty, the glorious sun is diving beneath the pool of heaven. Arise. The hour for your bath is slipping away." And the king went immediately to bathe.

The counsellor went home, still determined on his pilgrimage. He would not let his wife go with him, but started secretly. Not even his servants knew.

He wandered alone through many countries to many holy places, and finally came to the Odra country. There he saw a city near the ocean, where he entered a temple to Shiva and sat down in the court. There he sat, hot and dusty from long travel, when he was seen by a merchant named Treasure who had come to worship the god. The merchant gathered from his dress and appearance that he was a high-born Brahman, and invited him home, and entertained him with food, bathing, and the like.

When the counsellor was rested, the merchant asked him: "Who are you? Whence do you come? And where are you going?" And the other replied: "I am a Brahman named Farsight. I came here on a pilgrimage from the Anga country."

Then the merchant Treasure said to him: "I am preparing for a trading voyage to Golden Island. Do you stay in my house. And when I come back, and you are wearied from your pilgrimage, rest here for a time before going home." But Farsight said: "I do not want to stay here. I would rather go with you." And the good merchant agreed. And the counsellor slept in the first bed he had lain in for many nights.

The next day he went to the seashore with the merchant, and entered the ship loaded with the merchant's goods. He sailed along, admiring the wonders and terrors of the sea, till at last he reached Golden Island. There he stayed for a time until the merchant had finished his buying and selling. Now on the way back, he saw a magic tree suddenly rising from the ocean. It had beautiful branches, boughs of gold, fruits of jewels, and splendid blossoms. And sitting on a jewelled couch in the branches was a lovely maiden of heavenly beauty. And while the counsellor wondered what it all meant, the maiden took her lute in her hand, and began to sing:

Whatever seed of fate is sown, The fruit appears--'tis strange! Whatever deed a man has done, Not God himself can change.

And when she had made her meaning clear, the heavenly maiden straightway sank with the magic tree and the couch. And Farsight thought: "What a wonderful thing I have seen to-day! What a strange place the ocean is for the appearance of a tree with a fairy in it! And if this is a usual occurrence at sea, why do not other goddesses arise?"

The pilot and other sailors saw that he was astonished, and they said: "Sir, this wonderful maiden appears here regularly, and sinks a moment after, but the sight is new to you." Then the counsellor, filled with amazement, came to the shore with Treasure, and disembarked. And when the merchant had unloaded his goods and caused his servants to rejoice, the counsellor went home with him and spent many happy days there.

At last he said to Treasure: "Merchant, I have rested happily for a long time in your house. Now I wish to go to my own country. Peace be with you!" And in spite of urging from the merchant, Farsight took his leave, and started with no companion except his own courage. He went through many countries and at last reached the Anga country. And scouts who had been sent by King Glory-banner saw him before he reached the city. When the king learned of it, he went himself out of the city to meet him, for he had been terribly grieved by the separation. He drew near, embraced and greeted the counsellor and took him, all worn and dusty with the weary journey, into an inner room.

And as soon as the counsellor was refreshed, the king said: "Counsellor, why did you leave us? How could you bring yourself to do so harsh and loveless a thing? But after all, who can understand the strange workings of stern necessity? To think that you should decide all at once to wander off on a pilgrimage! Well, tell me what countries you visited, and what new things you saw."

Then the counsellor told him the whole story truthfully and in order, the journey to Golden Island and the fairy who rose singing from the sea, her wonderful beauty and the magic tree.

But the king immediately fell in love so hopelessly that his kingdom and his life seemed worthless to him without her. He took the counsellor aside and said: "Counsellor, I simply must see her. Remember that I shall die if I do not. I bow to my fate. I will take the journey which you took. You must not refuse me nor accompany me. I shall go alone and in disguise. You must rule the kingdom, and not dispute my words. Swear to do it on your life."

So he spoke, and would not listen to advice, but dismissed the counsellor. Then Farsight was unhappy though a great festival was made for him. How can a good counsellor be happy when his master devotes himself to a vice?

The next night King Glory-banner threw the burden of government on that excellent counsellor, assumed the dress of a hermit, and left his city. And as he travelled, he saw a monk named Grass, who said when the king bowed before him as a holy man: "My son, if you sail with a merchant named Fortune, you will obtain the maiden you desire. Go on fearlessly."

So the king bowed again and went on rejoicing. After crossing rivers and mountains he came to the ocean. And on the shore he met at once the merchant Fortune whom the monk had mentioned, bound for Golden Island. And when the merchant saw the king's appearance and his signet ring, he bowed low, took him on the ship, and set sail.

When the ship reached the middle of the sea, the maiden suddenly arose, sitting in the branches of the magic tree. And as the king gazed eagerly at her, she sang as before to her lute:

Whatever seed of fate is sown The fruit appears--'tis strange! Whatever deed a man has done, Not God himself can change.

Whatever, how, for whom, and where Tis fated so to be, That thing, just so, for him, and there Must happen fatally.

This song she sang, hinting at what was to happen. And the king gazed at her smitten by love, and could not move. Then he cried: "O Sea, in hiding her, you deceive those who think they have your treasures. Honour and glory to you! I seek your protection. Grant me my desire!" And as the king prayed, the maiden sank with the tree. Then the king jumped after her into the sea.

The good merchant Fortune thought he was lost and was ready to die of grief. But he was comforted by a voice from heaven which said: "Do nothing rash. There is no danger when he sinks in the sea. For he is the king Glory-banner, disguised as a hermit. He came here for the sake of the maiden; she was his wife in a former life. And he will win her and return to his kingdom in the Anga country." So the merchant sailed on to complete his business.

But King Glory-banner sank in the sea, and all at once he saw a heavenly city. He looked in amazement at the balconies with their splendid jewelled pillars, their walls bright with gold, and the network of pearls in their windows. And he saw gardens with pools that had stairways of various gems, and magic trees that yielded all desires. But rich as it was, the city was deserted.

He entered house after house, but did not find the maiden anywhere. Then he climbed a high balcony built of gems, opened a door, and entered. And there he saw her all alone, lying on a jewelled couch, and clad in splendid garments. He eagerly raised her face to see if it was really she, and saw that it was indeed the maiden he sought. At the sight of her he had the strange feeling of the traveller in a desert in summer at the sight of a river.

And she opened her eyes, saw that he was handsome and loveable, and left her couch in confusion. But she welcomed him and with downcast eyes that seemed like full-blown lotuses she did honour to his feet. Then she slowly spoke: "Who are you, sir? How did you come to this inaccessible under-world? And what is this hermit garb? For I see that you are a king. Oh, sir, if you would do me a kindness, tell me this."

And the king answered her: "Beautiful maiden, I am King Glory-banner of the Anga country, and I heard from a reliable person that you were to be seen on the sea. To see you I assumed this garb, left my kingdom, and followed you hither. Oh, tell me who you are."

Then she said to him with bashful love: "Sir, there is a king of the fairies named Moonshine. I am his daughter, and my name is Moonlight. Now my father has left me alone in this city. I do not know where he went with the rest of the people, or why. Therefore, as my home is lonely, I rise through the ocean, sit on a magic tree, and song about fate."

Then the king remembered the words of the monk, and urged her with such gentle, tender words that she confessed her love and agreed to marry him. But she made a condition: "My dear, on four set days in each month you must let me go somewhere unhindered and unseen. There is a reason." And the king agreed, married her, and lived in heavenly happiness with her.

While he was living in heavenly bliss, Moonlight said to him one day: "My dear, you must wait here. I am going somewhere on an errand. For this is one of the set days. While you stay here, sweetheart, you must not go into that crystal room, nor plunge into this pool. If you do, you will find yourself at that very moment in the world again." So she said good-bye and left the city.

But the king took his sword and followed, to learn her secret. And he saw a giant approaching with a great black cave of a mouth that yawned like the pit. The giant fell down and howled horribly, then took Moonlight into his mouth and swallowed her.

And the king's anger blazed forth. He took his great sword, black as a snake that has sloughed its skin, ran up wrathfully, and cut off the giant's head. He was blinded by his madness, he did not know what to do, he was afflicted by the loss of his darling. But Moonlight split open the stomach of the giant, and came out alive and unhurt, like the brilliant, spotless moon coming out from a black cloud.

When he saw that she was saved, the king cried: "Come, come to me!" and ran forward and embraced her. And he asked her: "What does it mean, dearest? Is this a dream, or an illusion?" And the fairy answered: "My dear, listen to me. It is not a dream, nor an illusion. My father, the king of the fairies, laid this curse upon me. My father had many sons, but he loved me so that he could not eat without me. And I used to come to this deserted spot twice a month to worship Shiva.

"One day I came here and it happened that I spent the whole day in worship. That day my father waited for me and would not eat or drink anything, though he was hungry and angry with me. At night I stood before him with downcast eyes, for I had done wrong. And he forgot his love and cursed me--so strong is fate. Because you have despised me and left me hungry a whole day, a giant named Terror-of-Fate will swallow you four times a month when you leave the city. And each time you will split him open and come out. And you shall not remember the curse afterwards, nor the pain of being swallowed alive. And you must live here alone.'

"But when I begged him, he thought awhile and softened his curse. When Glory-banner, King of the Angas, shall become your husband, and shall see you swallowed by the giant, and shall kill the giant, then the curse shall end, and you shall remember all your magic arts.' Then he left me here, and went with his people to the Nishadha mountain. But I stayed here because of the curse. And now the curse is ended, and I remember everything. So now I shall go to the Nishadha mountain to see my father. Of course now I remember how to fly. And you are at liberty to stay here, or to go back to your own kingdom."

Then the king was sad, and he begged her thus: "My beautiful wife, do not go for seven days. Be as kind as you are beautiful. Let me be happy with you in the garden, and forget my longings. Then you may go to your father, and I will go home." So he persuaded her, and was happy with her for six days in the garden. And the lilies in the ponds looked like longing eyes, and the ripples like hands raised to detain them, and the cries of swans and cranes seemed to say: "Do not leave us and go away."

On the seventh day the king cleverly led his wife to the pool from which one could get back to the world. There he threw his arms about her and plunged into the pool, and came up with her in the pool in the garden of his own palace.

The gardeners saw that the king had come back with a wife, and they joyfully ran and told the counsellor Farsight. He came and fell at the king's feet, and then led the king and the fairy into the palace. And the counsellor and the people thought: "Wonderful! The king has won the fairy whom others could see only for a moment like the lightning in the sky. Whatever is written in one's fate, that comes true, however impossible it may be."

But when Moonlight saw that the king was in his own country, and the seven days were over, she thought she would fly away like other fairies. But she could not remember how. Then she became very sad, like a woman who has been robbed.

And the king said: "Why are you so sad, my dear? Tell me." And the fairy said: "The curse is over. Yet because I have been bound so long in the fetters of your love, I have lost my magic arts. I cannot fly." Then the king thought: "The fairy is really mine," and he was happy and made a great feast.

When the counsellor Farsight saw this, he went home, and lay down on his bed, and his heart broke, and he died. Then the king governed the kingdom himself, and lived for a long time in heavenly happiness with Moonlight.

When he had told this story, the goblin said: "O King, when the king was so happy, why should the counsellor's heart break? Was it from grief because he did not win the fairy himself? Or from sorrow because the king came back, and he could no longer act as king? If you know and will not tell me, then you will lose your virtue, and your head will go flying into a hundred pieces."

And the king said to the goblin: "O magic creature, neither of these reasons would be possible for a high-minded counsellor. But he thought: The king used to neglect his duties for the sake of ordinary women. What will happen now, when he loves a fairy? In spite of all my efforts, a terrible misfortune has happened.' I think that was why his heart broke."

Then the magic goblin went back to his tree in a moment. And the king was still determined to catch him, and went once more to the sissoo tree.

The Brahman who died because Poison from a Snake in the Claws of a Hawk fell into a Dish of Food given him by a Charitable Woman
Who is to blame for his death?

Then the King went back under the sissoo tree, put the goblin on his shoulder, and started as before. And as he walked along, the goblin said to him again: "O King, listen to a very condensed story."

There is a city called Benares. In it lived a Brahman named Devaswami, whom the king honoured. He was very rich, and he had a son named Hariswami. This son had a wonderful wife, and her name was Beautiful. No doubt the Creator put together in her the priceless elements of charm and loveliness after his practice in making the nymphs of heaven.

One night Hariswami was sleeping on a balcony cooled by the rays of the moon. And a fairy prince named Love-speed was flying through the air, and as he passed he saw Beautiful asleep beside her husband. He took her, still asleep, and carried her off through the air.

Presently Hariswami awoke, and not seeing the mistress of his life, he rose in anxiety. And he wondered: "Oh, where has my wife gone? Is she angry with me? Or is she playing hide-and- seek with me, to see how I will take it?" So he roamed anxiously all over the balcony during the rest of the night. But he did not find her, though he searched as far as the garden.

Then he was overcome by his sorrow and sobbed convulsively. "Oh, Beautiful, my darling! Fair as the moon! White as the moonlight! Was the night jealous of your beauty; did she carry you away? Your loveliness shamed the moon who refreshed me with beams cool as sandal; but now that you are gone, the same beams torment me like blazing coals, like poisoned arrows!"

And as Hariswami lamented thus, the night came to an end, but his anguish did not end. The pleasant sun scattered the darkness, but could not scatter the blind darkness of Hariswami's madness. His pitiful lamentations increased a hundredfold, when the nightly cries of the birds ended. His relatives tried to comfort him, but he could not pluck up courage while his loved one was lost. He went here and there, sobbing out: "Here she stood. And here she bathed. And here she adorned herself. And here she played."

His relatives and friends gave him good advice. "She is not dead," they said. "Why should you make way with yourself? You will surely find her. Pluck up courage and hunt for her. Nothing is impossible to the brave and determined man." And when they urged him, Hariswami after some days plucked up heart.

He thought: "I will give all my fortune to the Brahmans, and then wander to holy places. Thus I will wear away my sins, and when my sins are gone, perhaps I shall find my darling in my wanderings." So he arose and bathed.

On the next day he provided food and drink, and made a great feast for the Brahmans, and gave them all he had except his piety. Then he started to wander to holy places, hoping to find his wife.

As he wandered, the summer came on him like a lion, the blazing sun its mouth, and the sunbeams its mane. And the hot wind blew, made hotter yet by the sighs of travellers separated from their wives. And the yellow mud dried and cracked, as if the lakes were broken-hearted at the loss of their lotuses. And the trees, filled with chirping birds, seemed to lament the absence of the spring, and their withering leaves seemed like lips that grow dry in the heat.

At this time Hariswami was distressed by the heat and the loss of his wife, by hunger, thirst, and weariness. And as he sought for food, he came to a village. There he saw many Brahmans eating in the house of a Brahman named Lotus-belly, and he leaned against the doorpost, speechless and motionless.

Then the good wife of that pious Brahman pitied him, and she thought: "Hunger is a heavy burden. It makes anyone light. Look at this hungry man standing with bowed head at the door. He looks like a pious man who has come from a far country, and he is tired. Therefore he is a proper person for me to feed."

So the good woman took in her hands a dish filled with excellent rice, melted butter, and candied sugar, and courteously gave it to him. And she said: "Go to the edge of our pond, and eat it."

He thanked her, took the dish, went a little way, and set it down under a fig-tree on the edge of the pond. Then he washed his hands and feet in the pond, rinsed his mouth, and joyfully drew near to eat the good food.

At that moment a hawk settled on the tree, carrying a black snake in his beak and claws. And the snake died in the grasp of the hawk, and his mouth opened, and a stream of poison came out. This poison fell into the dish of food.

But Hariswami did not see it. He came up hungry, and ate it all. And immediately he felt the terrible effects of the poison. He stammered out: "Oh, when fate goes wrong, everything goes wrong. Even this rice and the milk and the melted butter and the candied sugar is poison to me." And he staggered up to the Brahman's wife and said: "Oh, Brahman's wife, I have been poisoned by the food you gave me. Bring a poison-doctor at once. Otherwise you will be the murderer of a Brahman."

And the good woman was terribly agitated. But while she was running about to find a poison-doctor, Hariswami turned up his eyes and died. Thus, though she was not to blame, though she was really charitable, the poor wife reproached by the angry Brahman who thought she had murdered her guest. She was falsely accused for a really good action. So she was dejected and went on a pilgrimage.

When he had told this story, the goblin said: "O King, who murdered the Brahman? the snake, or the hawk, or the woman who gave him the food, or her husband? This was discussed in the presence of the god of death, but they could not decide. Therefore, O King, do you say. Who killed the Brahman? Remember the curse, if you know and do not tell the truth."

Then the king broke silence and said: "Who did the murder? The snake cannot be blamed, because he was being eaten by his enemy and could not help himself. The hawk was hungry and saw nothing. He was not to blame. And how can you blame either or both of the charitable people who gave food to a guest who arrived unexpectedly? They were quite virtuous, and cannot be blamed. I should say that the dead man himself was to blame, for he dared to accuse one of the others."

When the goblin heard this, he jumped from the king's shoulder and escaped to the sissoo tree. And the king ran after him again, determined to catch him.

The Girl who showed Great Devotion to the Thief.
Did he weep or laugh?

Then the king went back to the sissoo tree, put the goblin on his shoulder, and started. And as he walked along, the goblin said to him: "O King, I will tell you another story. Listen."

There is a city called Ayodhya, which was once the capital of Rama the exterminator of giants. In this city lived a strong-armed king named Hero-banner who protected the world as a wall protects a city. During his reign a great merchant named Jewel lived in the city. His wife was named Pleasing, and a daughter named Pearl was given to her prayers.

As the girl grew up in her father's house, her natural virtues grew too: beauty, charm, and modesty. And thus she became a young woman. Now in her young womanhood she was asked in marriage not only by great merchants, but even by kings. But she was prudent and did not like men. She would not have loved a god if he had been her husband. She was ready to die at merely hearing talk of her marriage. So her father was silent on the subject, though his tender love for her made him sad. And the story was known everywhere in Ayodhya.

At this time all the citizens were being plundered by thieves, and they petitioned King Hero-banner in these words: "O King, we are plundered every night by thieves, and cannot catch them. Your Majesty must decide what to do." So the king stationed night-watchmen in hiding about the city, to search out the thieves.

When the watchmen failed to catch the thieves for all their searching, the king himself took his sword, and wandered about alone at night. And he saw a man creeping along a wall with noiseless steps, often casting a fearful glance behind him. The king concluded that this was the thief who all alone robbed the city, and went up to him. And the thief asked him who he was. The king replied: "I am a thief."

Then the thief said joyfully: "Good! You are my friend. Come to my house. I will treat you like a friend." So the king agreed and went with the thief to a house hidden in a grove and guarded by a wall, full of delightful and beautiful things, and bright with shining gems. There the thief offered the king a seat, and went into an inner room.

At that moment a serving-maid came into the room and said to the king: "Your Majesty, why have you come into the jaws of death? This wonderful thief has gone out, intending to do you a mischief. He is certainly treacherous. Go away quickly."

So the king quickly went away, returned to the city, and drew up a company of soldiers. With these soldiers he went and surrounded the house where the serving-maid had been.

When the thief saw that the house was surrounded, he knew that he was betrayed, and came out to fight and die like a man. He showed more than human valour. He cut off the trunks of elephants, the legs of horses, and the heads of men; and he was all alone, with only his sword and shield. When the king saw that his army was destroyed, he ran forward himself.

The king was a scientific swordsman, so with a turn of his wrist he sent the sword and the dagger flying from the thief's hand. Then he threw away his own sword, wrestled with the thief, threw him, and took him alive.

The next morning the thief was led to the place of execution to be impaled, and the drums were beaten. And Pearl, the merchant's daughter, saw him from her balcony. All bloody and dusty as he was, she went mad with love, found her father, and said to him: "Father, I am going to marry that thief who is being led to execution. You must save him from the king. Otherwise I shall die with him."

But her father said: "What do you mean, my daughter? That thief stole everything the citizens had, and the king's men are going to kill him. How can I save him from the king? Besides, what nonsense are you talking?" But the more he scolded, the more determined she became. And as he loved his daughter, he went to the king and offered all he had for the release of the thief.

But the king would not be tempted by millions. He would not release the thief who stole everything, whom he had captured at the risk of his life. So the father returned home sadly. And the girl, not heeding the arguments of her relatives, took a bath, entered a litter, and went to the death-scene of the rogue, to die with him. Her parents and her relatives followed her, weeping.

At that moment the executioners impaled the thief. As his life ebbed away, he saw the girl and the people with her, and learned her story. Then the tears rolled down his cheeks, but he died with a smile on his lips.

The faithful girl took the thief's body from the stake, and mounted the pyre to burn herself. But the blessed god Shiva was staying invisibly in the cemetery, and at that moment he spoke from the sky: "O faithful wife, I am pleased with your constancy to the husband of your choice. Choose whatever boon you will from me."

The girl worshipped the gracious god and chose her boon: "O blessed one, my father has no son. May he have a hundred. Otherwise his childless life would end when I am gone."

And the god spoke again from the sky: "O faithful wife, your father shall have a hundred sons. But choose another boon. A woman faithful as you are deserves more than the little thing you asked."

Then she said: "O god, if I have won your favour, may this my husband live and always be a good man."

The invisible Shiva spoke from the sky: "So be it. Your husband shall be made alive and well. He shall be a good man, and King Hero-banner shall be pleased with him."

Then the thief arose at once, alive and well. And the merchant Jewel was overjoyed and astonished. He took Pearl and the thief, his son-in-law, went home with his rejoicing relatives, and made a feast great as his own delight, in honour of the sons he was to have.

And the king was pleased when he learned the story, and in recognition of the stupendous courage of the thief, he appointed him general at once. The thief reformed, married the merchant's daughter, and lived happily with her, devoted to virtue.

When the goblin had told this story, he reminded the king of the curse, and said: "O king, when the thief on the stake saw the merchant's daughter approaching with her father, did he weep or laugh? Tell me."

And the king answered: "He thought: I can make no return to this merchant for his unselfish friendship.' Therefore he wept from grief. And he also thought: Why does this girl reject kings and fall in love with a thief like me? How strange women are!' Therefore he laughed from astonishment."

When the goblin heard this, he immediately slipped from the king's shoulder and escaped to his home. But the king was not discouraged. He followed him to the sissoo tree.

The Man Who Changed Into a Woman at Will
Was his wife his or the other man's?

So the king went back as before under the sissoo tree, put the goblin on his shoulder, and started toward the monk. And as he walked along, the goblin told the king a story.

There was a city called Shivapur in Nepal. Long ago a king named Glory-banner lived there, and he deserved the name. He laid the burden of government on his counsellor named Ocean- of-Wisdom, and devoted himself to a life of pleasure with his wife Moonbright.

In course of time a daughter named Moonlight was born to them, pleasing as the moonlight to the eyes of men. When she grew up, she went one day in spring with her servants to a festival in the garden.

There she was seen by a Brahman youth named Master-mind, the son of Rich, who had come there to the festival. When he saw her plucking flowers with one arm uplifted, he went mad with love. His heart was taken captive by the gay maiden, and he was no longer master of his mind.

He thought: "Is she the goddess of love, plucking the spring flowers in person? Or is she a forest goddess, come here to worship the spring-time?"

Then the princess saw him, like a new god of love incarnate. The moment her eyes fell on him, she fell in love, forgetting her flowers and even her own limbs. While they looked at each other, lost in love like people in a picture, a great wail of anguish arose. They lifted their heads to learn what the matter was, and just then an elephant that had broken his chain, maddened by the scent of another mad elephant, came by, crushing the people in his path. He had thrown off his driver and the ankus hung from him as he ran. And everyone fled in terror.

But the youth Master-mind ran up in a hurry and took the princess in his arms. And with a mixture of fear and love and modesty she half embraced him as he carried her far out of the elephant's path. Then her people gradually gathered, and she went to the palace, looking at the youth, and burning over the flame of love.

And the youth went home from the garden, and thought: "I cannot live, I cannot exist a moment without her. I must seek help from my teacher Root, who is a thorough rogue." And so the day slowly passed.

The next morning he went to his teacher Root, and found him with his constant friend Moon. He drew near, bowed, and told his desire. And the teacher laughed and promised to help him.

So that wonderful rogue put a magic pill in his mouth, and thus changed himself into an old Brahman. He put a second pill into Master-mind's mouth, which changed him into a lovely girl. Then that prince of rogues took him to the king and said: "O King, this maiden has come a long distance to marry my only son. But my son has gone away, and I am going to look for him. Please keep the girl. For you are a protector to be trusted while I am looking for my son."

The king was afraid of a curse, so he promised to do it. And summoning his daughter, he said: "Daughter, keep this maiden in your chamber, and let her live with you." So the girl took the Brahman youth Master-mind in his girl form to her own apartments.

When Root had gone away, Master-mind in his girl form lived with his beloved, and in a few days came to know her in an intimate and loving way, as girl friends do. Then when he saw that she was pining away and tossing on her couch, he asked the princess one evening: "My dear girl, why do you grow pale and thin day by day, grieving as if separated from your love? Tell me. Why not trust a loving, innocent girl like me? If you will not tell me, I shall starve myself."

And the princess trusted him and said after a little hesitation: "My dear girl, why should I not trust you? Listen. I will tell you. One day I went to the spring festival in the garden. There I saw a handsome Brahman youth, fair as the moon but not so cold, the sight of whom kindled my love. For he adorned the garden as the spring-time does. While my eager eyes were feasting on his face, a great mad elephant that had broken his chain came charging and thundering past like a black cloud in the dry season. My servants scattered in terror, and I was helpless. But the Brahman youth took me in his arms and carried me far away. I seemed to be in a sandal bath, in a stream of nectar. I cannot tell how I felt as I touched him. Presently my servants gathered around, and I was brought here helpless. I felt as if I had fallen from heaven to earth. From that day I see in my thoughts my dear preserver beside me. I embrace him in my dreams. What need of more words? I wear away the time, thinking constantly of him and only him. The fire of separation from the lord of my life devours me day and night."

When Master-mind heard these welcome words, he rejoiced and counted himself happy. And thinking the time to reveal himself had come, he took the pill from his mouth, and disclosed his natural form. And he said: "Beautiful maiden, I am he whom you bought and enslaved with a kindly glance in the garden. I was sick at the separation from you; so I took the form of a girl, and came here. So now bring heaven in a loving glance to my love-tortured heart."

When the princess saw that the lord of her life was beside her, she was torn between love and wonder and modesty, and did not know what she ought to do. So they were secretly married and lived there in supreme happiness. Master-mind lived in a double form. By day he was a girl with the pill in his mouth, by night a man without the pill.

After a time the brother-in-law of King Glory-banner gave his daughter with great pomp to a Brahman, the son of the counsellor Ocean-of-Wisdom. And the princess Moonlight was invited to her cousin's wedding and went to her uncle's house. And Master-mind went with her in his girl form.

When the counsellor's son saw Master-mind in his lovely girl form, he was terribly smitten with the arrows of love. His heart was stolen by the sham girl, and he went home feeling lonely even with his wife. It made him crazy to think of that lovely face. When his father tried to soothe him, he woke from his madness and stammered out his insane desire. And his father was terribly distressed, knowing that all this depended on another.

Then the king learned the story and came there. When the king saw his condition and perceived that he was seven parts gone in love, he said: "How can I give him the girl who was intrusted to me by the Brahman? Yet without her he will be ten parts gone in love, and will die. And if he dies, then his father, the counsellor, will die too. And if the counsellor perishes, my kingdom will perish. What shall I do?"

He consulted his counsellors, and they said: "Your Majesty, the first duty of a king is the preservation of the virtue of his people. This is the fundamental principle, and is established as such among counsellors. If the counsellor is lost, the fundamental principle is lost; how then can virtue be preserved? So in this case it would be sinful to destroy the counsellor through his son. You must by all means avoid the loss of virtue which would ensue. Give the Brahman's girl to the counsellor's son. And when the Brahman returns, further measures will suggest themselves."

To this the king agreed, and promised to give the sham girl to the counsellor's son. So Master-mind in his girl form was brought from the chamber of the princess, and he said to the king: "Your Majesty, I was brought here by somebody for a given purpose. If you give me to somebody else, well and good. You are the king. Right and wrong depend on you. I will marry him to-day, but only on one condition. My husband shall go away immediately after the marriage and not return until he has been on a pilgrimage for six months. Otherwise I shall bite out my tongue."

So the counsellor's son was summoned, and he joyfully assented. He made the man his wife at once, put the sham wife in a guarded room and started on a pilgrimage. So Master-mind lived there in his woman form.

When he realized that the counsellor's son would soon return, Master-mind fled by night. And Root heard the story, and again assumed the form of an old Brahman. He took his friend Moon, went to Glory-banner, and said respectfully:

"Your Majesty, I have brought my son. Pray give me my daughter-in-law."

The king was afraid of a curse, so he said: "Brahman, I do not know where your daughter-in-law has gone. Be merciful. To atone for my carelessness, I will give your son my own daughter."

The prince of rogues in the form of an old Brahman angrily refused. But the king finally persuaded him, and with all due form married his daughter Moonlight to Moon, who pretended to be the old Brahman's son. Then Root went home with the bride and bridegroom.

But then Master-mind came, and in the presence of Root, a great dispute arose between him and Moon.

Master-mind said: "Moonlight should be given to me. I married the girl first with my teacher's permission."

Moon said: "Fool! What rights have you in my wife? Her father gave her to me in regular marriage."

So they disputed about the princess whom one had won by fraud and the other by force. But they could reach no decision.

O King, tell me. Whose wife is she? Resolve my doubts, and remember the agreement about your head.

Then the king said: "I think she is the rightful wife of Moon. For she was married to him in the regular way by her father in the presence of her relatives. Master-mind married her secretly, like a thief. And when a thief takes things from other people, it is never right."

When the goblin heard this, he went back home as before. And the king stuck to his purpose. He went back again, put the goblin on his shoulder, and started from the sissoo tree.

The Fairy Prince Cloud-chariot and the Serpent Shell-crest
Which is the more self-sacrificing?

So the king walked along with the goblin. And the goblin said: "O king, listen to a story the like of which was never heard."

There is a mountain called Himalaya where all gems are found. It is the king of mountains. Its proud loftiness is everywhere the theme of song. The sun himself has not seen its top.

On its summit is a city called Golden City, brilliant like a heap of sunbeams left in trust by the sun. There lived a glorious fairy-king named Cloud-banner. In the garden of his palace was a wishing-tree which had come down to him from his ancestors.

King Cloud-banner had worshipped the tree which was really a god, and by its grace had obtained a son named Cloud-chariot. This son remembered his former lives. He was destined to be a Buddha in a future life. He was generous, noble, merciful to all creatures, and obedient to his parents.

When he grew up, the king anointed him crown prince, persuaded thereto by his counsellors as well as by the remarkable virtues of the youth. While Cloud-chariot was crown prince, his father's counsellors came to him one day and kindly said: "Crown prince, you must always honour this wishing-tree in your garden; for it yields all desires, and cannot be taken away by anybody. As long as it is favourably disposed to us, the king of the gods could not conquer us, and of course nobody else could."

Then Cloud-chariot thought: "Alas! The men of old had this heavenly tree, yet they did not pluck from it any worthy fruit. They were mean-spirited. They simply begged it for some kind of wealth. And so they degraded themselves and the great tree too. But I will get from it the wish which is in my heart."

With this thought the noble creature went to his father. He showed such complete deference as to delight his father, then when his father was comfortably seated, he whispered: "Father, you know yourself that in this sea of life all possessions, including our own bodies, are uncertain as a rippling wave. Especially is money fleeting, uncertain, fickle as the twilight lightning. The only thing in life which does not perish is service. This gives birth to virtue and glory, twin witnesses through all the ages to come. Father! Why do we keep such a wishing-tree for the sake of transient blessings? Our ancestors clung to it, saying: It is mine, it is mine.' And where are they now? What is it to them, or they to it? Then, if you bid me, I will beg this generous wishing-tree for the one fruit that counts, the fruit of service to others."

His father graciously assented, and Cloud-chariot went to the wishing-tree, and said: "O god, you have fulfilled the wishes of our fathers. Fulfil now my one single wish. Remove poverty from the world. A blessing be with you. Go. I give you to the needy world." And as Cloud-chariot bowed reverently, there came a voice from the tree: "I go, since you give me up." And the wishing-tree immediately flew from heaven and rained so much money on the earth that nobody was poor. And Cloud-chariot's reputation for universal benevolence was spread about.

But all the relatives were jealous and envious. They thought that they could easily conquer Cloud-chariot and his father without the wishing-tree, and they prepared to fight to take away his kingdom. But Cloud-chariot said to his father: "Father, how can you take your weapons and fight? What high-minded man would want a kingdom after killing his relatives just for the sake of this wretched, perishable body? Let us abandon the kingdom, and go away somewhere to devote ourselves entirely to virtue. Then we shall be blessed in both worlds. And let these wretched relatives enjoy the kingdom which they hanker after."

And Cloud-banner said: "My son, I only want the kingdom for you, and if you give it up from benevolent motives, what good is it to me? I am an old man."

So Cloud-chariot left the kingdom and went with his father and mother to the Malabar hills. There he built a hermit's retreat, and waited on his parents.

One day, as he wandered about, he met Friend-wealth, the son of All-wealth, who lived there as king of the Siddhas. And Cloud-chariot spoke to him and made friends with him.

Then one day Cloud-chariot saw a shrine to the goddess Gauri in the grove, and entered there. And he saw a slender, lovely maiden surrounded by her girl friends and playing on a lute, in honour of Gauri. The deer listened to her music and her song, motionless as if ashamed because her eyes were lovelier than their own. When Cloud-chariot saw the slender maiden, his heart was ravished.

And he seemed to her to make the garden beautiful like the spring-time. A strange longing came over her. She became so helpless that her friends were alarmed.

Then Cloud-chariot asked one of her friends: "My good girl, what is your friend's sweet name? What family does she adorn?"

And the friend said: "This is Sandal, sister of Friend-wealth, and daughter of the king of the Siddhas." Then she earnestly asked for the name and family of Cloud-Chariot from a hermit's son who had come with him. And then she spoke to Sandal with words punctuated by smiles: "My dear, why do you not show hospitality to the fairy prince? He is a guest whom all the world would be glad to honour."

But the bashful princess remained silent with downcast eyes. Then the friend said: "She is bashful. Accept a hospitable greeting from me." And she gave him a garland.

Cloud-chariot, far gone in love, took the garland and put it around Sandal's neck. And the loving, sidelong glance which she gave him seemed like another garland of blue lotuses. So they pledged themselves without speaking a word.

Then a serving-maid came and said to the princess: "Princess, your mother remembers you. Come at once." And she went slowly, after drawing from her lover's face a passionate glance, for which Love's arrow had wedged a path.

And Cloud-chariot went to the hermitage, thinking of her; while she, sick with the separation from the lord of her life, saw her mother, then tottered to her bed and fell upon it. Her eyes were blinded as if by smoke from the fire of love within her, her limbs tossed in fever, she shed tears. And though her friends anointed her with sandal and fanned her with lotus-leaves, she found no rest on her bed or in the lap of a friend or on the ground.

Then when the day fled away with the passionate red twilight, and the moon drew near to kiss the face of the laughing East, she despaired of life, and her modesty would not let her send a message in spite of all her love. But somehow she lived through the night. And Cloud-chariot too was in anguish at the separation. Even in his bed he was fallen into the hand of Love. Though his passion was so recent, he had already grown pale. Though shame kept him silent, his looks told of the pangs of love. And so he passed the night.

In the morning he arose and went to the shrine of Gauri. And his friend, the hermit's son, followed him and tried to comfort him. At that moment the lovelorn Sandal came out of her house alone, for she could not endure the separation, and crept to that lonely spot to end her life there.

She did not see her lover behind a tree, and with eyes brimming with tears she prayed to the goddess Gauri: "O goddess, since I could not in this life have Cloud-chariot as my husband, grant that in another life at last he may be my husband."

Then she tied her garment to the limb of an ashoka tree before the goddess and cried: "Alas, my lord! Alas, Cloud-chariot! They say your benevolence is universal. Why did you not save me?"

But as she fastened the garment about her neck, a voice from the sky was heard in the air: "My daughter, do nothing rash. Cloud-chariot, the future king of the fairies, shall be your husband."

And Cloud-chariot heard the heavenly voice, and with his friend approached his rejoicing sweetheart. The friend said to the girl: "Here is the gift which the goddess grants you." And Cloud-chariot spoke more than one tender word and loosed the garment from her neck with his own hand.

Then a girl friend who had been gathering flowers there and had seen what was happening, came up joyfully and said, while Sandal's modest eyes seemed to be tracing a figure on the ground: "My dear, I congratulate you. Your wish is granted. This very day Prince Friend-wealth said in my presence to King All-wealth, your father: Father, the fairy prince , who deserves honour from all the world, who gave away the wishing-tree, is here, and we should treat him as an honoured guest. We could not find another bridegroom like him. So let us welcome him with the gift of Sandal who is a pearl of a girl.' And the king agreed, and your brother Friend-wealth has this moment gone to the hermitage of the noble prince. I think your marriage will soon take place. So go to your chamber, and let the noble prince go to his hermitage."

So she went slowly and happily and lovingly. And Cloud-chariot hastened to the hermitage. There he greeted Friend-wealth and heard his message, and told him about his own birth and former life. Then Friend-wealth was delighted and told Cloud-chariot's parents who were also delighted. Then he went home and made his own parents happy with the news.

That very day he invited Cloud-chariot to his home. And they made a great feast as was proper, and married the fairy prince and Sandal on the spot. Then Cloud-chariot was completely happy and spent some time there with his bride Sandal.

One day he took a walk for pleasure about the hills with Friend-wealth, and came to the seashore. There he saw great heaps of bones, and he asked Friend-wealth: "What creatures did these heaps of bones belong to?" His brother-in-law Friend-wealth said to the merciful prince: "Listen, my friend. I will tell you the story briefly."

Long ago Kadru, the mother of the serpents, made a wager with her rival Vinata, the mother of the great bird Garuda.

She won the wager and enslaved her rival. Now Garuda's anger continued even after he had freed his mother from slavery. He kept going into the underworld where Kadru's offspring, the serpents, live, to eat them. Some he killed, others he crushed.

Then Vasuki, king of the serpents, feared that in time all would be lost if the serpents were all to be slain thus. So he made an agreement with Garuda. He said: "O king of birds, I will send one serpent every day to the shore of the southern sea for you to eat. But you are never to enter the underworld again. What advantage would it be to you if all the serpents were slain at once?" And Garuda agreed, with an eye to his own advantage.

Since that time Garuda every day eats the snake sent by Vasuki here on the seashore. And these heaps of bones from the serpents that have been eaten, have in time formed a regular mountain.

When Cloud-chariot heard this story from the lips of Friend-wealth, he was deeply grieved and said: "My friend, wretched indeed is that king Vasuki who deliberately sacrifices his own subjects to their enemy. He is a coward. He has a thousand heads, yet could not find a single mouth to say: O Garuda, eat me first.' How could he be so mean as to beg Garuda to destroy his own race? Or how can Garuda, the heavenly bird, do such a crime? Oh, insolent madness!"

So the noble Cloud-chariot made up his mind that he would use his poor body that day to save the life of one serpent at least. At that moment a door-keeper, sent by Friend-wealth's father, came to summon them home. And Cloud-Chariot said: "Do you go first. I will follow." So he dismissed Friend-wealth, and remained there himself.

As he walked about waiting for the thing he hoped for, he heard a pitiful sound of weeping at a distance. He went a little way and saw near a lofty rock a sorrowful, handsome youth. He was at that moment abandoned by a creature that seemed to be a policeman, and was gently persuading his old, weeping mother to return. And Cloud-chariot wished to know who it might be. So he hid himself and listened, his heart melting with pity.

The old mother was bowed down by anguish, and started to lament over the youth. "Oh, Shell-crest! Oh, my virtuous son, whom I fondled, not counting the labour and the pain! Oh, my son, my only son! Where shall I see you again? Oh, my darling! When your bright face is gone, your old father will fall into black despair. How can he live then? Your tender form is hurt by the rays of the sun. How can it bear the pangs of being eaten by Garuda? Oh, my unhappy fate! Why did the Creator and the serpent-king choose my only son from the broad serpent-world, and seize upon him?"

And as she lamented, the youth, her son, said: "Mother, I am unhappy enough. Why torture me yet more? Return home. For the last time I bow before you. It is time for Garuda to come."

And the mother cried: "Alas, alas for me! Who will save my son?" And she gazed about wildly and wept aloud.

All this Cloud-chariot, the future Buddha, saw and heard. And with deep pity he thought: "Alas! This is a serpent named Shell-crest, sent here by Vasuki for Garuda to eat. And this is his mother, following him out of her great love. He is her only son, and she is mourning in pain and bitter anguish. I should forever curse my useless life if I did not save one in such agony at the cost of a body which must perish anyway some day."

So Cloud-chariot joyfully approached and said to the old mother: "Serpent-mother, I will save your son. Do not weep."

But the old mother thought that this was Garuda, and she screamed: "O Garuda, eat me! Eat me!"

Then Shell-crest said: "Mother, this is not Garuda. Do not be alarmed. What a difference between one who soothes our feelings like the moon, and the fearful Garuda."

And Cloud-chariot said: "Mother, I am a fairy, come to save your son. I will put on his garment and offer my own body to the hungry bird. Do you take your son and go home."

But the old mother said: "No, no. You are more than a son to me. To think that such as you should feel pity for such as we!"

And Cloud-chariot answered: "Mother, I beg you not to disappoint me." But when he insisted, Shell-crest said: "Noble being, you have certainly shown compassion, but I do not wish to save my body at the expense of yours. Who would save a common stone at the cost of a pearl? The world is full of creatures like me, who are merciful only to themselves. But creatures like you, who are merciful to all the world, are very rare. Oh, pious being, I could not stain the pure family of Shell-guard, as the dark spot stains the disk on the moon."

Then Shell-crest said to his mother: "Mother, return from this desolate place. Do you not see the rock of sacrifice wet with the blood of serpents, the terrible plaything of Death? I will go for a moment to the shore and worship the god Shiva there. And I will return quickly before Garuda comes."

So Shell-crest took leave of his mother and went to worship Shiva. And Cloud-chariot thought: "If Garuda should come in this interval, I should be happy."

Then he saw the trees stiffening themselves against the wind made by the sweeping wings of the king of birds. "Garuda is coming," he thought, and climbed the rock of sacrifice, eager to give his life for another.

And Garuda straightway pounced upon the noble creature and lifted him from the rock in his beak. While Cloud-chariot's blood flowed in streams and the gem fell from his forehead, Garuda carried him off and began to eat him on the summit of the Malabar hills. And while he was being eaten, Cloud-chariot thought: "In every future life of mine may my body do some good to somebody. I would not attain heaven and salvation without doing some good first." Then a shower of flowers fell from heaven on the fairy prince.

At that moment the blood-stained gem from his forehead fell in front of his wife Sandal. She was in anguish at the sight, and as her parents-in-law were near, she tearfully showed it to them. And they were alarmed at the sight of their son's gem and wondered what it meant. Then King

Cloud-banner discovered the truth by his magic arts, and he and his queen started to run with Cloud-chariot's wife Sandal.

At that moment Shell-crest returned from his worship of Shiva. He saw the rock stained with blood, and cried: "Alas for me, poor sinner! Surely that noble, merciful creature has given his body to Garuda in place of mine. I must find him. Where has the great being been carried by my enemy? If I find him alive, then I shall not sink into the slough of infamy." So he followed weeping the broad trail of blood.

Now Garuda noticed that Cloud-chariot was happy while being eaten, and he thought: "This must be some strange, great being, for he is happy while I am eating him. He does not die, and what remains of him is thrilled with delight. And he turns a gracious, benevolent look upon me. Surely, he is no serpent, but some great spirit. I will stop eating him and ask him."

But while he reflected, Cloud-chariot said: "O king of birds, why do you stop? There is still some flesh and blood on me, and I see that you are not satisfied. Pray continue to eat."

When the king of birds heard these remarkable words, he said: "You are no serpent. Tell me who you are."

But Cloud-chariot continued to urge him: "Certainly I am a serpent. What does the question mean? Continue your meal. What fool would begin a thing and then stop?"

At that moment Shell-crest shouted from afar: "O Garuda, do not commit a great and reckless crime. What madness is this? He is not a serpent. I am the serpent."

And he ran between them and spoke again to the agitated bird: "O Garuda, what madness is this? Do you not see that I have the hood and the forked tongue? Do you not see how gentle his appearance is?"

While he was speaking, Cloud-chariot's wife Sandal and his parents hurried up. And when his parents saw how he was lacerated, they wept aloud and lamented: "Alas, my son! Alas, Cloud-chariot! Alas for my merciful darling, who gave his life for others!"

But when they cried: "Alas, Garuda! How could you do this thoughtless thing?" then Garuda was filled with remorse and thought: "Alas! How could I be mad enough to eat a future Buddha? This must be Cloud-chariot, who gives his life for others, whose fame is trumpeted abroad through all the world. If he is dead, I am a sinner, and ought to burn myself alive. Why does the fruit of the poison-tree of sin taste sweet?"

While Garuda was thus deep in anxious thought, Cloud-chariot saw his relatives gathered, fell down, and died from the pain of his wounds. Then, while his grief-stricken parents were loudly lamenting, while Shell-crest was accusing himself, Sandal looked up to heaven and, in a voice stammering with tears, reproached the goddess Gauri who had graciously given her this husband: "Oh, Mother! You told me that the fairy prince should be my husband, but it is my fate that you spoke falsely."

Then Gauri appeared in a visible form, and said: "Daughter, my words are not false." And she sprinkled Cloud-chariot with nectar from a jar. And straightway he stood up alive, unhurt and more beautiful than before.

As they all bent low in worship, and Cloud-chariot rose only to bend again, the goddess said: "My son, I am pleased with your gift of your own body. With my own hand I anoint you king of the fairies." And she anointed Cloud-chariot with liquor from the jar, and then disappeared, followed by the worship of the company. And showers of heavenly blossoms fell from the sky, and the drums of the gods were joyfully beaten in heaven.

Then Garuda reverently said to Cloud-chariot: "O King, I am pleased with your more than human character. For you have done a strange thing of unparalleled nobility, to be marvelled at throughout the universe, to be written upon the walls of heaven. Therefore I am at your service. Choose from me what boon you will."

The noble creature said to Garuda: "O Garuda, you must repent and eat no more serpents. And you must restore to life those that you ate before, who now are nothing but bones."

And Garuda said: "So be it. I will eat no serpents hereafter. And those that I have eaten shall come to life."

Then all the serpents who had been eaten down to the bones, suddenly stood up. And through the grace of Gauri all the leading fairies learned immediately the wonderful deed of Cloud-chariot. So they all came and bowed at his feet and took him, freshly anointed by the very hand of Gauri, with his rejoicing relatives and friends to the Himalaya mountain. There Cloud-chariot lived happily with his father and his mother and his wife Sandal and Friend-wealth and the generous Shell-crest. And he ruled the fairy world radiant with gems.

When the goblin had told this long, strange story, he said to the king: "O King, tell me. Which was the more self-sacrificing, Cloud-chariot or Shell-crest? If you know and do not tell, then the curse I mentioned before will be fulfilled."

And the king said: "There was nothing remarkable in what Cloud-chariot did. He was prepared for it by the experiences of many past lives. But Shell-crest deserves praise. He was saved from death. His enemy had another victim, and was far away. Yet he ran after and offered his body to Garuda."

When the goblin heard this, he went back to the sissoo tree. And the king returned to catch him again.

The King who died for Love of his General's Wife; the General follows him in Death
Which is the more worthy?

Then the king went back under the sissoo tree, put the goblin on his shoulder as before, and started. And the goblin said to him: "O King, I will tell you another little story to relieve your weariness. Listen."

Long ago there was a city named Golden City on the bank of the Ganges, where a quarter of the old perfect virtue still lingers in these evil days. There was a king named Glorious, and he deserved the name. His bravery kept the world from being overflowed, like the shore of the sea.

In this king's city lived a great merchant, who had a daughter named Passion. Everyone who saw her fell in love and went mad with passion.

When she grew to be a young woman, the virtuous merchant went to King Glorious and said: "Your Majesty, I have a daughter, the gem of the three worlds, and she is old enough to marry. I could not give her to anyone without consulting your Majesty. For you are the master of all gems in the world. Pray marry her and thus lay me under obligations."

So the king sent his own Brahmans to examine her qualities. But when the Brahmans saw her supreme loveliness, they were troubled and thought: "If the king should marry her, his kingdom would be ruined. He would think only of her, and would doubtless neglect his kingdom. Therefore we must not report her good qualities to the king."

So they returned to the king and said: "Your Majesty, she has bad qualities." So the king did not marry the merchant's daughter. But he bade the merchant give his daughter to a general named Force. And she lived happily with her husband in his house.

After a time the lion of spring came dancing through the forest and slew the elephant of winter. And King Glorious went forth on the back of an elephant to see the spring festival. And the drum was beaten to warn virtuous women to stay within doors. Otherwise they would have fallen in love with his beauty, and love-sickness might be expected.

But when Passion heard the drum, she did not like to be left alone. She went out on the balcony, that the king might see her. She seemed like the flame of love which the spring-time was fanning with southern breezes. And the king saw her, and his whole being was shaken. He felt her beauty sinking deep in his heart like a victorious arrow of Love, and he fainted.

His servants brought him back to consciousness, and he returned to the city. There he made inquiries and learned that this was Passion whom he had rejected before. So he banished from the country the Brahmans who had said that she had bad qualities, and he thought longingly of her every day.

And as he thought of her, he burned over the flame of love, and wasted away day and night. And though from shame he tried to conceal it, he finally told the reason of his anguish to responsible people who asked him.

They said: "Do not suffer. Why do you not seize her?" But the virtuous king would not do it.

Then General Force heard the story. He came and bowed at the feet of the king and said: "Your Majesty, she is the wife of your slave, therefore she is your slave. I give her to you of my own accord. Pray take my wife. Or better yet, I will leave her here in the palace. Then you cannot be blamed if you marry her." And the general begged and insisted.

But the king became angry and said: "I am a king. How can I do such a wicked thing? If I should transgress, who would be virtuous? You are devoted to me. Why do you urge me to a sin which is pleasant for the moment, but causes great sorrow in the next world? If you abandon your wedded wife, I shall not pardon you. How could a man in my position overlook such a transgression? It is better to die." Thus the king argued against it. For the truly great throw away life

rather than virtue. And when all the citizens came together
and urged him, he was steadfast and refused.

So he slowly shrivelled away over the fever-flame of love
and died. There was nothing left of King Glorious except his
glory. And the general could not endure the death of his king.
He burned himself alive. The actions of devoted men are
blameless.

When the goblin on the king's shoulder had told this story,
he asked the king: "O King, which of these two, the king and
the general, was the more deserving? Remember the curse
before you answer."

The king said: "I think the king was the more deserving."

And the goblin said reproachfully: "O King, why was not
the general better? He offered the king a wife like that, whose
charms he knew from a long married life. And when his king
died, he burned himself like a faithful man. But the king gave
her up without really knowing her attractions."

Then the king laughed and said: "True enough, but not
surprising. The general was a gentleman born, and acted as
he did from devotion to his superior. For servants must
protect their masters even at the cost of their own lives. But
kings are like mad elephants who cannot be goaded into
obedience, who break the binding-chain of virtue. They are
insolent, and their judgment trickles from them with the holy
water of consecration. Their eyes are blinded by the
hurricane of power, and they do not see the road. From the
most ancient times, even the kings who conquered the world
have been maddened by love and have fallen into misfortune.
But this king, though he ruled the whole world, though he
was maddened by the girl Passion, preferred to die rather
than set his foot on the path of iniquity. He was a hero. He
was the better of the two."

Then the goblin escaped by magic from the king's shoulder
and went back. And the king pursued him, undiscouraged. No
great man stops in the middle of the hardest undertaking.

The Youth who went through the Proper Ceremonies
Why did he fail to win the magic spell?

Then the king went back through the night to the cemetery filled with ghouls, terrible with funeral piles that seemed like ghosts with wagging tongues of flame. But when he came to the sissoo tree, he was surprised to see a great many bodies hanging on the tree. They were all alike, and in each was a goblin twitching its limbs.

And the king thought: "Ah, what does this mean? Why does that magic goblin keep wasting my time? For I do not know which of all these I ought to take. If I should not succeed in this night's endeavour, then I would burn myself alive rather than become a laughing-stock."

But the goblin understood the king's purpose, and was pleased with his character. So he gave up his magic arts. Then the king saw only one goblin in one body. He took him down as before, put him on his shoulder, and started once more.

And as he walked along, the goblin said: "O King, if you have no objections, I will tell you a story. Listen."

There is a city called Ujjain, whose people delight in noble happiness, and feel no longing for heaven. In that city there is real darkness at night, real intelligence in poetry, real madness in elephants, real coolness in pearls, sandal, and moonlight.

There lived a king named Moonshine. He had as counsellor a famous Brahman named Heaven-lord, rich in money, rich in piety, rich in learning. And the counsellor had a son named Moon-lord.

This son went one day to a great resort of gamblers to play. There the dice, beautiful as the eyes of gazelles, were being thrown constantly. And Calamity seemed to be looking on, thinking: "Whom shall I embrace?" And the loud shouts of angry gamblers seemed to suggest the question: "Who is there that would not be fleeced here, were he the god of wealth himself?"

This hall the youth entered, and played with dice. He staked his clothes and everything else, and the gamblers won it all. Then he wagered money he did not have, and lost that. And when they asked him to pay, he could not. So the gambling-master caught him and beat him with clubs.

When he was bruised all over by the clubs, the Brahman youth became motionless like a stone, and pretended to be dead, and waited. After he had lain thus for two or three days, the heartless gambling-master said to the gamblers: "He lies like a stone. Take him somewhere and throw him into a blind well. I will pay you the money he owes."

So the gamblers picked Moon-lord up and went far into the forest, looking for a well. Then one old gambler said to the others: "He is as good as dead. What is the use of throwing him into a well now? We will leave him here and go back and say we have left him in a well." And all the rest agreed, and left him there, and went back.

When they were gone, Moon-lord rose and entered a deserted temple to Shiva. When he had rested a little there, he thought in great anguish: "Ah, I trusted the rascally gamblers, and they cheated me. Where shall I go now, naked and dusty as I am? What would my father say if he saw me now, or any relative, or any friend? I will stay here for the present, and at night I will go out and try to find food somehow to appease my hunger."

While he reflected in weariness and nakedness, the sun grew less hot and disappeared. Then a terrible hermit named Stake came there, and he had smeared his body with ashes. When he had seen Moon-lord and asked who he was and heard his story, he said, as the youth bent low before him: "Sir, you have come to my hermitage, a guest fainting with hunger. Rise, bathe, and partake of the meal I have gained by begging."

Then Moon-lord said to him: "Holy sir, I am a Brahman. How can I partake of such a meal?"

Then the hermit-magician went into his hut and out of tenderness to his guest he thought of a magic spell which grants all desires. And the spell appeared in bodily form, and said: "What shall I do?" And the hermit said: "Treat that man as an honoured guest."

Then Moon-lord was astonished to see a golden palace rise before him and a grove with women in it. They came to him from the palace and said: "Sir, rise, come, bathe, eat, and meet our mistress." So they led him in and gave him a chance to bathe and anoint himself and dress. Then they led him to another room.

There the youth saw a woman of wonderful beauty, whom the Creator must have made to see what he could do. She rose and offered him half of her seat. And he ate heavenly food and various fruits and chewed betel leaves and sat happily with her on the couch.

In the morning he awoke and saw the temple to Shiva, but the heavenly creature was gone, and the palace, and the women in it. So he went out in distress, and the hermit in his hut smiled and asked him how he had spent the night. And he said: "Holy sir, through your kindness I spent a happy night, but I shall die without that heavenly creature."

Then the hermit laughed and said: "Stay here. You shall have the same happiness again to-night." So Moon-lord enjoyed those delights every night through the favour of the hermit.

Finally Moon-lord came to see what a mighty spell that was. So, driven on by his fate, he respectfully begged the hermit: "Holy sir, if you really feel pity for a poor suppliant like me, teach me that spell which has such power."

And when he insisted, the hermit said: "You could never win the spell. One has to stand in the water to win it. And it weaves a net of magic to bewilder the man who is repeating the words, so that he cannot win it. For as he mumbles it, he seems to lead another life, first a baby, then a boy, then a youth, then a husband, then a father. And he falsely imagines that such and such people are his friends, such and such his enemies. He forgets his real life and his desire to win the spell. But if a man mumbles it constantly for twenty-four years, and remembers his own life, and is not deceived by the network of magic, and then at the end burns himself alive, he comes out of the water, and has real magic power. It comes only to a good pupil, and if a teacher tries to teach it to a bad pupil, the teacher loses it too. Now you have the real benefit through my magic power. Why insist on more? If I lost my powers, then your happiness would go too."

But Moon-lord said: "I can do anything. Do not fear, holy sir." And the hermit promised to teach him the spell. What will holy men not do out of regard to those who seek aid?

So the hermit went to the river bank, and said: "My son, mumble the words of the spell. And while you are leading an imaginary life, you will at last be awakened by my magic. Then plunge into the magic fire which you will see. I will stand here on the bank while you mumble it."

So he purified himself and purified Moon-lord and made him sip water, and then he taught him the magic spell. And Moon-lord bowed to his teacher on the bank, and plunged into the river.

And as he mumbled the words of the spell in the water, he was bewildered by its magic. He forgot all about his past life, and went through another life. He was born in another city as the son of a Brahman. Then he grew up, was consecrated, and went to school. Then he took a wife, and after many experiences half pleasant, half painful, he found himself the father of a family. Then he lived for some years with his parents and his relatives, devoted to wife and children, and interested in many things.

While he was experiencing all these labours of another life, the hermit took pity on him and repeated magic words to enlighten him. And Moon-lord was enlightened in the midst of his new life. He remembered himself and his teacher, and saw that the other life was a network of magic. So he prepared to enter the fire in order to win magic power.

But older people and reliable people and his parents and his relatives tried to prevent him. In spite of them he hankered after heavenly pleasures, and went to the bank of a river where a funeral pile had been made ready. And his relatives went with him. But when he got there he saw that his old parents and his wife and his little children were weeping.

And he was perplexed, and thought: "Alas! If I enter the fire, all these my own people will die. And I do not know whether my teacher's promise will come true or not. Shall I go into the fire, or go home? No, no. How could a teacher with such powers promise falsely? Indeed, I must enter the fire." And he did.

And he was astonished the feel the fire as cool as snow, and lost his fear of it. Then he came out of the water of the river, and found himself on the bank. He saw his teacher standing there, and fell at his feet, and told him the whole story, ending with the blazing funeral pile.

Then his teacher said: "My son, I think you must have made some mistake. Otherwise, why did the fire seem cool to you? That never happens in the winning of this magic spell."

And Moon-lord said: "Holy sir, I do not remember making any mistake." Then his teacher was eager to know about it, so he tried to remember the spell himself. But it would not come to him or to his pupil. So they went away sad, having lost their magic.

When the goblin had told this story, he asked the king: "O King, explain the matter to me. Why did they lose their magic, when everything had been done according to precept?"

Then the king said: "O magic creature, I see that you are only trying to waste my time. Still, I will tell you. Magic powers do not come to a man because he does things that are hard, but because he does things with a pure heart. The Brahman youth was defective at that point. He hesitated even when his mind was enlightened. Therefore he failed to win the magic. And the teacher lost his magic because he taught it to an unworthy pupil."

Then the goblin went back to his home. And the king ran to find him, never hesitating.

The Boy whom his Parents, the King, and the Giant conspired to Kill

Why did he laugh at the moment of death?

Then the king went to the sissoo tree, put the goblin on his shoulder as before, and started in silence. And the goblin on his shoulder saw that he was silent and said: "O King, why are you so obstinate? Go home. Spend the night in rest. You ought not to take me to that rascally monk. But if you insist, then I will tell you another story. Listen."

There is a city called Brilliant-peak. There lived a glorious king named Moon, who delighted the eyes of his subjects. Wise men said that he was brave, generous, and the very home of beauty. But in spite of all his wealth, he was very sad at heart. For he found no wife worthy of him.

One day this king went with soldiers on horseback into a great wood, to hunt there and forget his sorrow. There he split open many boars with his arrows as the sun splits the black darkness, and made fierce lions into cushions for his arrows, and slew mountainous monsters with his terrible darts.

As he hunted, he spurred his horse and beat him terribly. And the horse was so hurt by the spur and the whip that he could not tell rough from smooth. He dashed off quicker than the wind, and in a moment carried the king into another forest a hundred miles away.

There the king lost his way, and as he wandered about wearily, he saw a great lake. He stopped there, unsaddled his horse, let him bathe and drink, and found him some grass in the shade of the trees. Then he bathed and drank himself, and when he had rested, he looked all about him.

And he saw a hermit's daughter of marvellous beauty under an ashoka tree with another girl. She had no ornaments but flowers. She was charming even in a dress of bark. She was particularly attractive because of her thick masses of hair arranged in a girlish way.

And the king fell in love with her and thought: "Who is she? Is she a goddess come to bathe in these waters? Or Gauri, separated from her husband Shiva, leading a hard life to win him again? Or the lovely moon, taking a human form, and trying to be attractive in the daytime? I will go to her and find out."

So he drew near to her. And when she saw him coming, she was astonished at his beauty and dropped her hands, which had been weaving a garland of flowers. And she thought: "Who can he be in this forest? Some fairy perhaps. Blessed are my eyes this day."

So she rose, modestly looking another way, and started to go away, though her limbs failed her. Then the king approached and said: "Beautiful maiden, I have come a long distance, and you never saw me before. I ask only to look at you, and you should welcome me. Is this hermit manners, to run away?"

Then her clever friend made the king sit down and treated him as an honoured guest. And the king respectfully asked her: "My good girl, what happy family does your friend adorn? What are the syllables of her name, which must be a delight to the ear? Or why at her age does she torture a body as delicate as a flower with a hermit's life in a lonely wood?"

And the friend answered: "Your Majesty, she is the daughter of the hermit Kanva and the heavenly nymph Menaka. She grew up here in the hermitage, and her name is Lotus-bloom. With her father's permission she came here to the lake to bathe. And her father's hermitage is not far from here."

Then the king was delighted. He mounted his horse and rode to the hermitage of holy Kanva, to ask for the girl. And he entered the hermitage in modest garb, leaving his horse outside. Then he was surrounded by hermits with hoary crowns and bark garments like the trees, and saw the sage Kanva radiant and cool like the moon. And he drew near and fell at his feet.

And the wise hermit greeted him and let him rest, then said: "My son Moon, I will tell you something to your advantage. Listen. I know what fear of death there is in mortal creatures. Why then do you uselessly kill the wild beasts? Warriors were made by the Creator to protect the timid. Therefore protect your subjects in righteousness, and root out evil. As Happiness flees before you, strive to overtake her with all your means, elephants and horses and things. Enjoy your kingship. Be generous. Become glorious. Abandon this vice of hunting, this sport of Death. For slayer and slain are equally deceived. Why spend your time in such an evil pursuit?"

The sensible king was pleased and said: "Holy sir, I am instructed. And great is my gratitude for this instruction. From now on I hunt no more. Let the wild animals live without fear."

Then the hermit said: "I am pleased with your protection of the animals. Choose any boon you will."

Then the quick-witted king said: "Holy sir, if you are kindly disposed, give me your daughter Lotus-bloom."

So the hermit gave him his daughter, the child of the nymph, who then came up after her bath. So they were married, and the king wore cheerful garments, and Lotus-bloom was adorned by the hermits' wives. And the weeping hermits accompanied them in procession to the edge of the hermitage. Then the king took his wife Lotus-bloom, mounted his horse, and started for his city.

At last the sun, seeing the king tired with his long journeying, sank wearily behind the western mountain. And fawn-eyed night appeared, clad in the garment of darkness, like a woman going to meet her lover. And the king saw an ashvattha tree on the shore of a pond in a spot covered with grass and twigs, and he decided to spend the night there.

So he dismounted, fed and watered his horse, brought water from the pond, and rested with his beloved. And they passed the night there.

In the morning he arose, performed his devotions, and prepared to set out with his wife to rejoin his soldiers. Then, like a cloud black as soot with tawny lightning-hair, there appeared a great giant. He wore a chaplet of human entrails, a cord of human hair, he was chewing the head of a man, and drinking blood from a skull.

The giant laughed aloud, spit fire in his wrath, and showed his dreadful fangs. And he scolded the king and said: "Scoundrel! I am a giant named Flame-face. This tree is my home; even the gods do not dare to trespass here. But you and your wife have trespassed and enjoyed yourselves. Now swallow your own impudence, you rascal! You are lovesick, so I will split open your heart and eat it, and I will drink your blood."

The king was frightened when he saw that the giant was invincible, and his wife was trembling, so he said respectfully: "I trespassed ignorantly. Forgive me. I am your guest, seeking protection in your hermitage. And I will give you a human sacrifice, so that you will be satisfied. Be merciful then and forget your anger."

Then the giant forgot his anger, and thought: "Very well. Why not?" And he said: "O King, I want a noble, intelligent Brahman boy seven years old, who shall give himself up of his own accord for your sake. And when he is killed, his mother must hold his hands tightly to the ground, and his father must hold his feet, and you must cut off his head with your own sword. If you do this within seven days, then I will forgive the insult you have offered me. If not, I will kill you and all your people."

And the king was so frightened that he consented. Then the giant disappeared.

Then King Moon mounted his horse with his wife Lotus-bloom and rode away sad at heart, seeking for his soldiers. And he thought: "Alas! I was bewildered by hunting and by love, and I find myself ruined. Where can I find such a sacrifice for the giant? Well, I will go to my own city now, and see what happens."

So he continued his search, and found his soldiers and his city Brilliant-peak. There his subjects were delighted because he had found a wife worthy of him, and they made a great feast. But it was a day of despondency and dreadful agony for the king.

On the next day he told his counsellors the whole story. And one counsellor named Wise said: "Your Majesty, do not despair. I will find a victim for the sacrifice. The world is a strange place."

Thus the counsellor comforted the king, and made a statue of a boy out of gold. And he sent the statue about the land, with constant beating of drums and this proclamation: "We want a noble Brahman boy seven years old who will offer himself as a sacrifice to a giant with the permission of his parents. And when he is killed, his mother must hold his hands, and his father must hold his feet. And as a reward, the king will give his parents a hundred villages and this statue of gold and gems."

Now there was a Brahman boy on a farm, who was only seven years old, but wonderfully brave. He was of great beauty, and even in childhood he was always thinking about others. He said to the heralds: "Gentlemen, I will give you my body. Wait a moment. I will hurry back after telling my parents."

So they told the boy to go. And he went into the house, bowed before his parents, and said: "Mother! Father! I am going to give this wretched body of mine in order to win lasting happiness. Pray permit me. And I will take the king's gift, this statue of myself made of gold and gems, and give it to you together with the hundred villages. Thus I will pay my debt to you, and do some real good. And you will never be poor again, and will have plenty more sons."

But his parents immediately said: "Son, what are you saying? Have you the rheumatism? Or are you possessed by a devil? If not, why do you talk nonsense? Who would sacrifice his child for money? And what child would give his body?"

But the boy said: "I am not mad. Listen. My words are full of sense. The body is the seat of unnameable impurities, it is loathsome and full of pain. It perishes in no long time at best. If some good can be done with the worthless thing, that is a great advantage in this weary life, so wise men say. And what good is there except helping others? If anyone can serve his parents so easily, then how lightly should the body be esteemed!"

Thus the boy, with his bold words and his firm purpose, persuaded his grieving parents. And he went and got from the king's men the golden statue and the hundred villages, and gave them to his parents.

So the boy with his parents followed the king's men to the city Brilliant-peak. And the king looked upon the brave boy as a magic jewel for his own preservation, and rejoiced greatly. He adorned the boy with garlands and perfumes, put him on an elephant, and took him with his parents to the home of the giant.

There the priest traced a magic circle beside the tree, and reverently lit the holy fire. Then the horrible giant Flame-face appeared, mumbling words of his own. He staggered, for he was drunk with blood, and snorted and yawned. His eyes flashed fire and his shadow made the whole world dark.

And the king said respectfully: "Great being, here is the human sacrifice you asked for, and this is the seventh day since I promised it. Be merciful. Accept this sacrifice."

And the giant licked his chops, and looked the boy over, who was to be the sacrifice. Then the noble boy thought: "I have done some good with this body of mine. May I never rest in heaven or in eternal salvation, but may I have many lives in which to do some good with my body." And the air was filled with the chariots of gods who rained down flowers.

Then the boy was laid before the giant. His mother held his hands, and his father held his feet. When the king drew his sword and was ready to strike, the boy laughed so heartily that all of them, even the giant, forgot what they were doing, looked at the boy's face, and bowed low before him.

When the goblin had told this strange story, he asked the king: "O King, why did the boy laugh at the moment of death? I have a great curiosity about this point. If you know and will not tell, then your head will fly into a hundred pieces."

And the king said: "Listen. I will tell you why the boy laughed. When danger comes to any weak creature, he cries for life to his mother and father. If they are not there, he begs protection from the king, whom heaven made his protector. Failing the king, he cries to a god. Some one of these should be his protector. But in the case of this boy everything was contrary. His parents held his hands and feet because they wanted money. And the king was ready to kill him with his own hand, to save his own life. And the giant, who is a kind of a god, had come there especially to eat him. So the boy thought: They are ridiculously fooled about their bodies, which are fragile, worthless, the seat of pain and suffering. The bodies of the greatest gods perish. And such creatures as these imagine that their bodies will endure!' So when he saw their strange madness, and felt that his own wishes were fulfilled, the Brahman boy laughed in astonishment and delight."

Then the goblin slipped from the king's shoulder and went back to his home. And the king followed with determination. The heart of a good man is like the heart of the ocean. It cannot be shaken.

The Man, his Wife, and her Lover, who all died for Love
Which was the most foolish?

Then the king went back under the sissoo tree, took the goblin on his shoulder, and set out in haste. And as he walked along, the goblin on his shoulder said: "O King, I will tell you a story about a great love. Listen."

There is a city called Ujjain, which seems like a divine city made by the Creator for the pious who have fallen from heaven. In this city there was a famous king named Lotus-belly. He delighted the good, and defeated the king of the demons.

While he was king, a merchant named Fortune, richer than the god of wealth, lived in the city. He had one daughter named Love-cluster, who seemed the model from whom the Creator had made the nymphs of heaven. This merchant gave his daughter to a merchant named Jewel-guard from Copper City.

As he was a tender father and had no other children, the merchant stayed with his daughter Love-cluster and her husband. Now Love-cluster came to hate Jewel-guard as a sick man hates a pungent, biting medicine. But the beautiful woman was dearer than life to her husband, dear as long-fathered wealth to a miser.

One day Jewel-guard started for Copper City to pay a loving visit to his parents. Then the hot summer came, and the roads were blocked for travellers by the sharp arrows of the sun. The winds blew soft with the fragrance of jasmine and trumpet-flower, like sighs from the mouths of mountains separated from the springtime. And wind-swept dust-clouds flew to the sky like messengers from the burning earth begging for clouds. And the feverish days moved slowly like wayfarers who cling to the shade of trees. And the nights clad in pale yellow moonlight became very feeble without the invigorating embrace of winter.

At this time Love-cluster, anointed with cooling sandal, and clad in thin garments stood at her lattice-window. And she saw a handsome youth with a friend whom he trusted. He seemed the god of love born anew and seeking his bride. He was the son of the king's priest, and his name was Lotus-lake.

And when Lotus-lake saw the lovely girl, he expanded with delight as lotuses in a lake expand at the sight of the moon. When the two young people saw each other, their hearts embraced each other at the bidding of Love, their teacher.

So Lotus-lake was smitten with love, and was led home with difficulty by his friend. And Love-cluster was equally maddened by love. First she learned from her friend his name and home, then slowly withdrew to her room. There she thought of him and became feverish with love, simply tossing on her couch, seeing nothing and hearing nothing.

After two or three days spent in this way, she felt bashful and fearful, pale and thin from the separation, and hopeless of union with her lover. So, as if drawn on by the moonbeam which shone through her window, she went out at night when her people were asleep, determined to die. And she came to a pool under a tree in her garden.

There stood a family image of the goddess Gauri, set up by her father. She drew near to this image, bowed before the goddess, praised her, and said: "O Goddess, since I could not have Lotus-lake as my husband in this life, may he be my husband in some other life!" And she made a noose of her garment, and tied it to the ashoka tree before the goddess.

At that moment her trusty friend awoke, and not finding her in the room, hunted about and came luckily into the garden. There she saw the girl fastening the noose about her neck, and she cried, "No, no!" And running up, she cut the noose.

When Love-cluster saw that it was her own friend who had run up and taken the noose away, she fell to the ground in great agony. But her friend comforted her and asked the reason of her sorrow. Then she arose and said: "Jasmine, my friend, I cannot be united with him I love. I am dependent on my father and other people. Death is the happiest thing for me."

And as she spoke, she was terribly scorched by the fiery darts of love, and determined to feel no more hope, and fainted. And her friend Jasmine lamented: "Alas! Love is a hard master. It has reduced her to this condition." But she gradually brought her back to life with cool water and fans and things. She made an easy bed of lotus-leaves. She put pearls cool as snow on her heart.

Then Love-cluster came to herself and slowly said to her weeping friend: "My dear, the fire within me cannot be quenched by such things as pearls. If you want to save my life, be clever enough to bring my lover to me."

And the loving Jasmine said: "My dear, the night is almost over. In the morning I will bring your lover here to meet you. Be brave and go now to your room."

Love-cluster was contented. She took the pearls from her neck and gave them to her friend as a present. And she said: "Let us go now. Then in the morning you must keep your promise." So she went to her room.

In the morning Jasmine crept out without being seen to hunt for the house of Lotus-lake. When she got there, she found Lotus-lake under a tree in the garden. He was lying on a couch of lotus-leaves moistened with sandal, and the friend who knew his secret was fanning him with plantain-leaf fans, for he was tortured by the flames of love. And Jasmine hid, to find out whether this was lovesickness for her friend or not.

Then the friend said to Lotus-lake: "My friend, comfort your heart by glancing a moment at this charming garden. Do not be so troubled."

But he said to his friend: "My heart has been stolen by Love-cluster. It is no longer in my body. How can I comfort it? Love has made an empty quiver of me. So invent some plan by which I may meet the thief of my heart."

Then Jasmine came out joyfully and without fear and showed herself. And she said: "Sir, Love-cluster has sent me to you, and I am the bearer of a message to you. Is it good manners to enter the heart of an innocent girl by force, steal her thoughts, and run away? It is strange, but the sweet girl is ready to give her person and her life to you, her charmer. For day and night she heaves sighs hot as the smoke from the fire of love that burns in her heart. And teardrops carry her rouge away and fall, like bees longing for the honey of her lotus-face. So, if you wish it, I will tell you what is good for both of you."

And Lotus-lake said: "My good girl, the words which tell me that my love is lonely and longing, frighten me and comfort me. You are our only refuge. Devise a plan."

And Jasmine answered: "This very night I will bring Love-cluster secretly to the garden. You must be outside. Then I will cleverly let you in, and so you two will be united." Thus Jasmine delighted the Brahman's son, and went away successful to please Love-cluster with the news.

Then the sun and the daylight fled away, pursuing the twilight. And the East adorned her face with the moon. And the white night-blooming lotuses laughed, their faces expanding at the thought of the glory that was coming to them. At that hour the lover Lotus-lake came secretly, adorned and filled with longing, to the garden-gate of his beloved. And Jasmine led Love-cluster secretly into the garden, for she had lived through the day somehow.

Then Jasmine made her sit down under the mango trees, while she went and let Lotus-lake in. So he entered and looked upon Love-cluster as the traveller looks upon the shade of trees with thick foliage. And as he drew near, she saw him and ran to him, for love took away her modesty, and she fell on his neck. "Where would you go? I have caught you, thief of my heart!" she cried. Then excessive joy stopped her breathing and she died. She fell on the ground like a vine broken by the wind. Strange are the mysterious ways of Love.

When Lotus-lake saw that terrible fall, he cried: "Oh, what does it mean?" And he fainted and fell down. Presently he came to himself, and took his darling on his lap. He embraced her and kissed her and wept terribly. He was so borne down by the terrible burden of grief that his own heart broke. And when they were both dead, the night seemed to die away in shame and fear.

In the morning the relatives heard the story from the gardeners, and came there filled with timidity and wonder and grief and madness. They did not know what to do, but stood a long time with downcast eyes. Unfaithful women disgrace a family.

Presently the husband Jewel-guard came back from his father's house in Copper City, filled with love for Love-cluster. When he came to his father-in-law's house and saw the business, he was blinded by tears and went thoughtfully into the garden. There he saw his wife dead in another man's arms, and his body was scorched by flames of grief, and he died immediately.

Then the whole household shouted and screamed so that all the citizens heard the story and came there. The demi-gods themselves were filled with pity and prayed to the goddess Gauri whose image had been set up there before by Love-cluster's father: "Oh, Mother, the merchant who set up this statue was always devoted to you. Show mercy to him in his affliction."

And the gracious goddess heard their prayer. She said: "All three shall live again, and shall forget their love." Then through her grace they all arose like people waking from sleep. They were alive, and their love was gone. While all the people there rejoiced at what had happened. Lotus-lake went home, bending his head in shame. And the merchant took his shamefaced daughter and her husband and went into the house and made a feast.

When the goblin had told this story on the road in the night, he said: "O King, which was the most foolish among those who died for love? If you know and do not tell, you must remember the curse I spoke of before."

Then the king answered: "O magic creature, Jewel-guard was the most foolish of them. When he saw that his wife had died for love of another man, he should have been angry. Instead, he was loving, and died of grief."

Then the goblin slipped from the king's shoulder and quickly set out for his home. And the king ran after him again, eager as before.

The Four Brothers who brought a Dead Lion to Life
Which is to blame when he kills them all?

Then the king went back to the sissoo tree, took the goblin, put him on his shoulder, and started for the place he wished to reach. And as he walked along the road, the goblin began to talk again: "Bravo, King! You are a remarkable character. So I will tell you another story, and a strange one. Listen."

There is a city called Flower-city. There lived a king named Earth-boar. In his kingdom was a farm where a Brahman lived whose name was Vishnuswami. His wife was named Swaha. And four sons were born to them.

After a time the father died, and the relatives took all the money. So the four brothers consulted together: "There is nothing for us to do here. Suppose we go somewhere." And after a long journey they came to the house of their maternal grandfather in a village called Sacrifice. The grandfather was dead, but their uncles sheltered them, and they continued their studies.

But they did not amount to much, so in time their uncles became scornful in such matters as food and clothing. And they were troubled.

Then the eldest took the others aside and said: "Brothers, no man can do anything anywhere on earth. Now I was wandering about discouraged, and I came to a wood. There I saw to-day a dead man whose limbs lay relaxed on the ground. And I wished for the same fate, and I thought: He is happy. He is free from the burden of woe.' So I made up my mind to die, and hanged myself with a rope from a tree. I lost consciousness, but before the breath of life was gone, the cord was cut and I fell to the ground. And when I came to myself, I saw a compassionate man who had happened by at that moment, and he was fanning me with his garment. And he said to me: My friend, you are an educated man. Tell me why you are so despondent. The righteous man finds happiness, the unrighteous man finds unhappiness because of his unrighteousness, and for no other reason. If you made up your mind to this because of unhappiness, practice righteousness instead. Why seek the pains of hell by suicide?' Thus the man comforted me and went away. And I gave up the idea of suicide and came here. You see I could not even die when fate was unwilling. Now I shall burn my body at some holy place, that I may not again feel the woes of poverty."

Then the younger brothers said to him: "Sir, why is an intelligent man sad for lack of money? Do you not know that money is uncertain as an autumn cloud? No matter how carefully won and guarded, three things are fickle and bring sorrow at the last: evil friendships, a flirt, and money. The resolute and sensible man should by all means acquire that virtue which brings him Happiness a captive in bonds."

So the eldest brother straightway plucked up heart, and said: "What virtue is it which we should acquire?"

Then they all reflected, and took counsel together: "We will wander over the earth, and each of us will learn some one science." So they appointed a place for meeting, and the four brothers started in four different directions.

After a time they all gathered at the meeting-place, and asked one another what they had learned. The first said: "I have learned a science by which I can take the skeleton of any animal whatever and put the proper kind of flesh on it."

The second said: "I have learned a science by which I can put on the flesh-covered skeleton the proper hair and skin."

The third said: "My science is this. When the skin and the flesh and the hair are there, I can put in the eyes and the other organs of sense."

The fourth said: "When the organs are there, I can give the creature the breath of life."

So all four went into the forest to find a skeleton and test their various sciences. As fate would have it, they found the skeleton of a lion there. And they took that, not knowing the difference.

The first fitted out the skeleton with appropriate flesh. The second added the skin and hair. The third provided all the organs. The fourth gave life to the thing, and it was a lion. The lion arose with terrible massive mane, dreadful teeth in his mouth, and curving claws in his paws. He arose and killed his four creators, then ran into the forest.

Thus the Brahman youths all perished because they did wrong to make a lion. Who could expect a good result from creating a bad-tempered creature? Thus, if fate opposed, even a virtue that has been painfully acquired does not profit, but rather injures. But the tree of manhood, with the water of intelligence poured into its watering-trench of conduct about the vigorous root of fate, generally bears good fruit.

When the goblin had told this story, he asked the king who was walking through the night: "O King, remember the curse I mentioned, and tell me which of them was most to blame for creating the lion?"

And the king reflected in silence: "He wants to escape again. Very well. I will catch him again." So he said: "The one who gave life to the lion, is the sinner. The others did not know what kind of an animal it was, and just showed their skill in creating flesh and skin and hair and organs. They were not to blame because they were ignorant. But the one who saw that it was a lion and gave it life just to exhibit his skill, he was guilty of the murder of Brahmans."

Then the goblin went home. And the king followed him again, and came to the sissoo tree.

The Old Hermit who exchanged his Body for that of the Dead Boy
Why did he weep and dance?

Then the king went back to the sissoo tree, put the goblin on his shoulder in spite of all its writhings, and set out in silence. And the goblin on his shoulder said: "O king of kings, you are terribly obstinate about this impossible task. So to amuse the weary journey I will tell a story. Listen."

In the Kalinga country was a city called Beautiful, where people lived as happily as in heaven. There ruled a famous king named Pradyumna. And in a part of this city was a region set apart by the king, where many Brahmans lived. Among them was a learned, wealthy, pious, hospitable Brahman named Sacrifice.

In his old age a single son was born to him and his worthy wife. The boy grew under the fostering care of his father, and showed signs of excellence. He was called Devasoma by his father, and his parents were entirely devoted to him.

In his sixteenth year the boy attracted everyone by his learning and modesty. Then he suddenly fell ill of a fever and died. When his father and mother saw that he was really dead, they embraced the body and wept aloud. But their love for him would not permit them to burn the body.

So the old relatives gathered, and said to the father: "Brahman, life is imaginary like a city in the sky. Do you not know this, you who know things above and things below? The kings who enjoyed themselves like gods upon the earth, they have gone one by one to cemeteries filled with processions of weeping ghosts. Their bodies were burned by the flesh-devouring fire and eaten by jackals. No one could prevent it in their case. How much less in the case of others? Therefore, as you are a wise man, tell us what you mean by embracing this dead body?"

So at last the relatives persuaded him to let his son go, and they put the body in a litter and brought it to the cemetery with weeping and wailing.

At that time a hermit was fulfilling a hard vow, and was living in a hut in the cemetery. He was very thin because of his age and his hard life. His veins stuck out like cords to bind him, as if afraid that he would break in pieces. His hair was tawny like the lightning.

This hermit heard the wailing of the people, and turned to his pupil who begged food for him. Now this pupil was proud and arrogant. And the hermit said: "My boy, what is this wailing we hear? Go outside and find out, then return and tell me why this unheard-of commotion is taking place."

But the pupil said: "I will not go. Go yourself. My hour for begging is passing by."

Then the teacher said: "Fool! Glutton! What do you mean by your hour for begging? Only one half of the first watch of the day is gone."

Then the bad pupil became angry and said: "Decrepit old man! I am not your pupil. And you are not my teacher. I am going away. Do your begging yourself." And he angrily threw down his staff and bowl before the old man, and got up, and went away.

Then the hermit laughed. He left his hut and went to the place where the dead Brahman boy had been brought to be burned. He saw how the people mourned over such youthful freshness dead, and felt his own age and weakness. So he made up his mind to exchange his body for the other by magic.

He went aside and wept at the top of his voice. Then he danced with all the proper gestures.

After that, full of the longing to enjoy the happiness of youth, he left his own withered body by magic and entered the body of the Brahman youth. So the Brahman youth came to life on the funeral pyre and stood up. And a cry of joy arose from all the relatives: "See! The boy is alive! He is alive!"

Then the magician in the body of the Brahman boy said to the relatives: "I went to the other world, and Shiva gave me life and directed me to perform a great vow. So now I am going off to perform the vow. If I do not, my life will not last. Do you then go home, and I will come later."

So he spoke to those gathered there, having made up his mind what to do, and sent them home full of joy and grief. He went himself and threw his old body into a pit, and then went off, a young man.

When the goblin had told this story, he said to King Triple-victory, who was walking through the night: "O King, when the magician entered another person's body, why did he weep before doing it, or why did he dance? I have a great curiosity about this point."

And the king was afraid of the curse, so he broke silence and said: "Listen, goblin. He thought: I am leaving to-day this body with which I won magic powers, the body which my parents petted when I was a child.' So first he wept from grief, and from love of his body which he found it hard to leave. Then he thought: With a new body I can learn more magic.' So he danced from joy at getting youth."

When the goblin heard this answer, he returned quickly to the sissoo tree. And the king pursued him, undismayed.

The Father and Son who married Daughter and Mother
What relation were their children?

The king paid no attention to the terrible witch of night, clad in black darkness, with the funeral piles as flaming eyes. He bravely went through the dreadful cemetery to the sissoo tree, put the goblin on his shoulder, and started as before. And as he walked along, the goblin said to him: "O King, I am very tired with these comings and goings, but you do not seem to be. So I will tell you my Great Puzzle. Listen."

Long ago there was a king named Virtue in the southern country. He was the best of righteous men, and was born in a great family. His wife came from the Malwa country, and her name was Moonlight. And they had one daughter, whom they named Beauty.

When this daughter was grown up, the relatives conspired to wreck the kingdom and drive King Virtue out. But he escaped by night, took a great many jewels, and fled from his kingdom with his beautiful wife and his daughter. He started for his father-in-law's house in Malwa, and came with his wife and daughter to the Vindhya forest. There they spent a weary night.

In the morning the blessed sun arose in the east, stretching out his rays like hands to warn the king not to go into the forest where robbers lived. The king went on foot with his trembling daughter and his wife, and their feet were wounded by the thorny grass. So they came to a fortified village. It was like the city of Death; for there were no righteous people there, and it was filled with robber-men who killed and robbed other people.

As the king drew near with his fine garments and his gems, many robbers saw him from a distance, and ran out armed to rob him. When the king saw them coming, he said to his wife and daughter: "These are wild men. They must not touch you.

Go into the thick woods." So the queen with her daughter Beauty fled in fear into the middle of the forest.

But the brave king took his sword and shield and killed many of the wild men as they charged down, raining arrows on him. Then their leader gave an order, and all the robbers fell on the king at once, wounded every limb in his body, and killed him; for he was all alone. So the robbers took the jewels and went away.

Now the queen had hidden in a thicket, and had seen her husband killed. Then she fled a long distance in fear and came with her daughter into another thick wood. The rays of the midday sun were so fierce that travellers had to sit in the shade. So Queen Moonlight and Princess Beauty sat down under an ashoka tree near a lotus-pond in terrible weariness and fear and grief.

Now a gentleman named Fierce-lion who lived near came on horseback with his son into that wood to hunt. The son's name was Strong-lion. And the father saw the footprints of the queen and the princess, and he said to his son: "My son, these footprints are clean-cut and ladylike. Let us follow them. And if we find two women, you shall marry one of them, whichever you choose."

And the son Strong-lion said: "Father, the one who has the little feet in this line of footprints, seems to be the wife for me. The one with the bigger feet must be older. She is the wife for you."

But Fierce-lion said: "My son, what do you mean? Your mother went to heaven before your eyes. When so good a wife is gone, how could I think of another?"

But his son said: "Not so, Father. A householder's house is an empty place without a wife. Besides, you have surely heard what the poet says:

What fool would go into a house? Tis a prisoner's abode, Unless a buxom wife is there, Looking down the road.'

So, Father, I beg you on my life to marry the second one, whom I have chosen for you."

Then Fierce-lion said "Very well," and went on slowly with his son, following the footprints. And when he came to the pond, he saw Queen Moonlight, radiant with beauty and charm. And with his son he eagerly approached her. But when she saw him, she rose in terror, fearing that he was a robber.

But her sensible daughter said: "There is no reason to fear. These two men are not robbers. They are two well-dressed gentlemen, who probably came here to hunt." Still the queen swung in doubt.

Then Fierce-lion dismounted and stood before her. And he said: "Beautiful lady, do not be frightened. We came here to hunt. Pluck up heart and tell me without fear who you are. Why have you come into this lonely wood? For your appearance is that of ladies who wear gems and sit on pleasant balconies. And why should feet fit to saunter in a court, press this thorny ground? It is a strange sight. For the wind-blown dust settles on your faces and robs them of beauty. It hurts us to see the fierce rays of the sun fall upon such figures. Tell us your story. For our hearts are sadly grieved to see you in such a plight. And we cannot see how you could live in a forest filled with wild beasts."

Then the queen sighed, and between shame and grief she stammered out her story. And Fierce-lion saw that she had no husband to care for her. So he comforted her and soothed her with tender words, and took care of her and her daughter. His son helped the two ladies on horseback and led them to his own city, rich as the city of the god of wealth. And the queen seemed to be in another life. She was helpless and widowed and miserable. So she consented. What could she do, poor woman?

Then, because the queen had smaller feet, the son Strong-lion married Queen Moonlight. And Fierce-lion, the father, married her daughter, the princess Beauty, because of the bigness of her feet. Who would break a promise that had been made solemnly?

Thus, because of their inconsistent feet, the daughter became the wife of the father and the mother-in-law of her own mother. And the mother became the wife of the son and the daughter-in-law of her own daughter. And as time passed, sons and daughters were born to each pair.

When the goblin had told this story, he asked the king: "O King, when children were born to the father and daughter, and other children to the son and mother, what relation were those children to one another? If you know and do not tell, then remember the curse I spoke of before?"

When the king heard the goblin's question, he turned the thing this way and that, but could not say a word. So he went on in silence. And when the goblin saw that he could not answer the question, he laughed in his heart and thought: "This king cannot give an answer to my Great Puzzle. So he just walks on in silence. And he cannot deceive me because of the power of the curse. Well, I am pleased with his wonderful character. So I will cheat that rogue of a monk, and give the magic power he is striving after to this king."

So the goblin said aloud: "O King, you are weary with your comings and goings in this dreadful cemetery in the black night, yet you seem happy, and never hesitate at all. I am astonished and pleased at your perseverance. So now you may take the dead body and go ahead. I will leave the body. And I will tell you something that will do you good, and you must do it. The monk for whom you are carrying this body, is a rogue. He will call upon me and worship me, and he will try to kill you as a sacrifice. He will say: Lie flat on the ground in an attitude of reverence.' O King, you must say to that rascal: I do not know this attitude of reverence. Show me first, and then I will do likewise.' Then when he lies on the ground to show you the attitude of reverence, cut off his head with your sword. Then you will get the kingship over the fairies which he is trying to get. Otherwise, the monk will kill you and get the magic power. That is why I have delayed you so long. Now go ahead, and win magic power."

So the goblin left the body on the king's shoulder and went away. And the king reflected how the monk Patience was planning to hurt him. He took the body and joyfully went to the fig-tree.

CONCLUSION

So King Triple-victory came to the monk Patience with the body on his shoulder. And he saw the monk along in the dark night, sitting under the cemetery tree and looking down the road. He had made a magic circle with yellow powdered bones in a spot smeared with blood. In it he had put a jug filled with blood and lamps with magic oil. He had kindled a fire and brought together the things he needed for worship.

The monk rose to greet the king who came carrying the body, and he said: "O King, you have done me a great favour, and a hard one. This is a strange business and a strange time and place for such as you. They say truly that you are the best of kings, for you serve others without thinking of yourself. This is the very thing that makes the greatness of a great man, when he does not give a thing up, though it costs his very life."

So the monk felt sure the he was quite successful, and he took the body from the king's shoulder. He bathed it and put garlands on it, and set it in the middle of the circle. Then he smeared his own body with ashes, put on a cord made of human hair, wrapped himself in dead man's clothes, and stood a moment, deep in thought. And the goblin was attracted by his thought into the body, and the monk worshipped him.

First he offered liquor in a skull, then he gave him human teeth carefully cleaned, and human eyes and flesh. So he completed his worship, then he said to the king: "O King, fall flat on the ground before this master magician in an attitude of reverence, so that he may give you what you want."

And the king remembered the words of the goblin. He said to the monk: "Holy sir, I do not know that attitude of reverence. Do you show me first, and afterwards I will do it in the same way."

And when the monk fell on the ground to show the attitude of reverence, the king cut off his head with a sword, and cut out his heart and split it open. And he gave the head and the heart to the goblin.

Then all the little gods were delighted and cried: "Well done!" And the goblin was pleased and spoke to the king from the body he was living in: "O King, this monk was trying to become king of the fairies. But you shall be that when you have been king of the whole world."

And the king answered the goblin: "O magic creature, if you are pleased with me, I have nothing more to wish for. Yet I ask you to make me one promise, that these twenty-two different, charming puzzle-stories shall be known all over the world and be received with honour."

And the goblin answered: "O King, so be it. And I will tell you something more. Listen. When anyone tells or hears with proper respect even a part of these puzzle-stories, he shall be immediately free from sin. And wherever these stories are told, elves and giants and witches and goblins and imps shall have no power."

Then the goblin left the dead body by magic, and went where he wanted to. Then Shiva appeared there with all the little gods, and he was well pleased. When the king bowed before him, he said: "My son, you did well to kill this sham monk who tried by force to become king of the fairies. Therefore you shall establish the whole earth, and then become king of the fairies yourself. And when you have long enjoyed the delights of heaven and at last give them up of your own accord, then you shall be united with me. So receive from me this sword called Invincible. While you have it, everything you say will come true."

So Shiva gave him the magic sword, received his flowery words of worship, and vanished with the gods.